MY ETERNAL LOVE

LORD OF THE HUNT   **THE TULPA KNIGHT**

STEP IN TIME

JULIET CARDIN

This is a work of fiction. Names, characters, places, and incidents are products of the author's imagination or are used fictitiously and are not to be construed as real. Any resemblance to actual events, locations, organizations, or persons, living or dead, is entirely coincidental.

World Castle Publishing, LLC

Pensacola, Florida

Copyright © 2024 Juliet Cardin

Paperback ISBN: 9798891262669

eBook ISBN: 9798891262676

First Edition World Castle Publishing, LLC, September 29, 2024

http://www.worldcastlepublishing.com

Licensing Notes

Cover: Karen Fuller

Editor: Karen Fuller

LORD

OF THE

HUNT

PROLOGUE
LORD OF THE HUNT

For generations, the men of the Cole family bloodline have turned into wolves. Balen Cole has relentlessly searched for an end to the transformation. He becomes especially desperate when his betrothed arrives earlier than expected, seeking his protection.

Alena Harford had to rush to Balen's side when another man sought to claim her as his own. Though she has heard the dark rumors about the Cole family, Alena is willing to risk anything to be Balen's bride. She plays the role of a delicate lady, but she isn't as helpless as she leads others to believe.

The pair finds love and desire in each other's arms. But how long can they hope to survive when a vile menace arrives, threatening to expose their secrets and endangers their very lives?

CHAPTER 1

LORD OF THE HUNT

Balen followed the tantalizing smell of old, rotting foliage spread across the forest floor. Years of footsteps from forest animals, horses, and men all lay before him. Every leaf, stick, and stone told a story. A veritable scent smorgasbord.

Twinkling stars and a glowing orb moon lit up the woods, though his enhanced sight needed no aid. This was his land, home to his kind for generations. Miles and miles surrounded Terron Castle, which perched high upon a cliff looking down to the ground below.

A trail wound through the trees, taking him deeper into the thick woods, until it widened and met up with the lone, narrow track upon which horse and coach could fit. An unfamiliar odor invaded his nostrils. The sound of wolves fresh for the hunt urged him onward.

Ahead, the flicker of torchlight reflected erratically among the trees. Shouts of men, screams of horses, and a woman pounded in his ears. The wolves were attacking. Over a dozen of them circled in on their prey who stood terrified and uncertain on the dark road.

"Damn you, beasts!" yelled the coachman.

"Spread out," a rider commanded.

A shot exploded, then three more.

Balen crouched at the edge of the forest, counting the men, following sight of the wolves. Six guardsmen all together. They were outnumbered, but all of them were armed. Another shot blasted, and he heard a wolf yelp in agony. The wolves bared their teeth and circled in and out of the trees, taunting the men.

The coach bore the insignia of a falcon with a white rose grasped in its talons. The scent of a lone female reached Balen's nose.

No!

His muscles flexed in frustration. She should not be here now. It was too early. He hadn't expected her for another three days.

He threw his head back and howled.

Answering calls soon sounded all around him. With cautious steps, he crept forward. Three wolves were close to the men, unwilling to give ground. All the other wolves, hearing the order of their leader, threaded into the woods and away.

A slope allowed one of the remaining animals to leap to the top of the coach. Another jumped up, and the first one leaped for the driver's throat. More shots rang out.

"Don't fire upon the coach! You'll kill her!" shouted one of the guards.

They trained their weapons instead upon the wolf struggling on the ground with the driver. The man was dead, his throat ripped out. The wolf lifted its huge, black head and displayed its bloodied fangs.

Caleb, no! You fool!

A succession of shots flew, raining on the bloodied wolf. He soon lay dead beside his kill.

The coach door flung wide, and a woman scrambled out. "It's coming in through the roof!" she cried.

Balen stared upward and saw the other black wolf scratching and gnawing at the thin wood, snapping the ceiling of the coach.

Damn it! Why did they not leave at my command?

The woman reached for an abandoned torch, no longer lit, and flung it wildly around her, desperate to keep the danger away. The flow of her long, blonde hair spread out, whipping around her like the cloak she wore. Her porcelain face glowed beneath the moon, and he caught sight of the fear in her huge, blue eyes.

So beautiful.

He threw his head back and howled again. The spot where he stood was exposed, and a shot fired in his direction. Easily, he dodged the deadly bullet. He lowered his head and growled. The threat of the two wolves was great. Risking himself, Balen ran forward and leaped into the air. Shots flew at him as he smashed into the wolf just as it dove from atop the coach toward the guards. He could imagine the thoughts coursing through the men at the sight of the two wolves, one black as night, the other shimmering silver. They were well matched, both thickly muscled, vicious, angry beasts. What the men didn't know was where one fought for blood lust, the other fought for love.

"Stop!" the woman screamed. "The silver wolf, it's fighting the black. Aim your weapons at that other one."

Balen knew she meant the lone wolf pacing in and out of the woods. He snarled and bit and struggled with the black wolf. His teeth gripped the back of its neck, battling for dominance. He had to hurry. He knew there was one more threat on the loose. With no other choice, he spun the wolf over onto its back and clamped down on its throat, closing his eyes and shuddering as he felt its life slip away.

Shouts from the men spurred him into action again. He took in the scene and saw the danger at once. The woman struggled with the last wolf, who had taken advantage of the chaos. It caught the torch she waved and fought her for it. The men yelled and scrambled around, desperate to help, but couldn't fire their weapons for fear they would hit the lady.

"Let go!" insisted one of the guards.

"If she lets go, it'll be on her," another argued.

"It'll rip her throat out," said another.

Balen gauged the men.

One of them saw him standing over his bloodied kill and gestured to the others. "Look! He's killed the other wolf."

"See the color of him. By God, I'd swear he shimmers like an angel."

"Maybe he's here to help?" a young fellow suggested hopefully.

"Back up," the man who appeared to be in command ordered.

The men obeyed and lowered their weapons a fraction.

Balen took the cue and leaped, teeth bared, at the last wolf. He caught it off-guard, ramming against its shoulder, spinning it around, away from the woman. She backed up, the torch tight in her hands.

This wolf was also black, huge, and fierce. Balen wanted no more death, having already fought and killed one of his own. His sharp teeth and iron jaw clamped down on the beast, he used his strength to throw the animal several feet. It landed hard on its side but was up again in an instant, shaking its head. Balen lowered his head and growled as they faced off.

Leave, Tristan!

After what seemed like an eternity, the black wolf threw back its head and howled before it turned and ran. Balen watched him go, then turned back to face the travelers.

Weapons were lifted and aimed at him now. He moved back, head high, showing he was no threat.

"Go on, get!" the commander yelled at him. He lowered his weapon.

When all guns lowered except one, Balen moved toward the forest.

"No!" he heard the woman cry out. "Leave him be."

He reached the line of trees and turned. The woman stood between him and the threat. He darted for cover and ran.

Terron soon came into sight. He trotted up the long, winding roadway toward the formidable structure. Around back, he headed for the door that led to the kitchen. Frantically, he scratched at the heavy wood. The door cracked open, and he darted inside, past the startled old woman, and moved through the keep.

Once he reached the chamber at the top of the tower, he bolted through the entrance and urged the door shut with his snout. He came up before the hearth and laid down, panting heavily by the warm fire. Closing his eyes, he took deep breaths and concentrated.

The change came quickly. There was no pain.

Once his transformation was complete, Balen rose wearily to his feet. He stood before the fire, staring into the depths of the flames. A knock sounded at the door. Naked, he turned.

A dark-haired man of equal height to

Balen entered the room. Dressed all in black, his white teeth gleamed in the firelight.

"Are you all right?" the man asked, eyes sparkling wickedly.

Balen moved to the pile of clothing nearby and began to dress. "Yes. No thanks to you. What the devil were you thinking, Tristan?"

"The men were eager for the hunt."

"We don't hunt people. Or have you forgotten?"

"It was only in sport," Tristan argued, quick with an easy smile.

Balen shoved his foot into a high black boot and glared at him. "Tell that to Caleb or to the others who lay dead."

The smile froze on Tristan's face. "An unfortunate hazard of our lives."

Fully dressed, Balen reached for his cloak. "It did not have to happen. Do you know who you attacked on the road tonight?"

Tristan shrugged. "Travelers. Of no consequence."

Balen strode toward the chamber door, paused, and turned. "That was Lady Alena Harford out there. My betrothed." He slammed the door on his way out.

* * * *

Alena sat forward on her seat in the coach, peering intently at the castle perched upon the hilltop ahead. Her arrival was early and unexpected, and she didn't know what kind of welcome she could expect to receive. The hour was late. The moon had risen high in the sky, and here she came, arriving like a thief in the night.

The coach rolled beneath the raised portcullis that, a hundred years ago, would have been staunchly closed and guarded. Ahead loomed the small but imposing castle. It was said to be three hundred years old. She saw the glow of candlelight up in the single tower and through a few windows on each of the three floors. At least someone was awake.

When they drew up before the massive, arched, double doors, she heard one of her party climb down from the coach. The unfortunate death of her original driver stirred an ache of regret in her belly. It was her fault—all of this. The desperate need to leave her home and venture here early had come quite unexpectedly. The route was long, however, and she'd hoped to travel at leisure and arrive at the scheduled date. Things hadn't turned out that way.

The coach door opened, and Alena

reached out to the guard to help her down. Another of the guards had dismounted and now went up before the great entranceway. He pounded on the heavy wood, and moments later, one door creaked open. An elderly man, standing very erect, dressed as a butler, stepped out. He noted the coach and smiled at Alena.

"Lady Harford? What a pleasant surprise. We weren't expecting you until the end of the week."

Alena smiled back at him. "I'm so sorry to arrive early—Timms, is it?"

He inclined his head. "No need for apology, my lady. Lord Cole will be glad to see you."

Lord Balen Cole was her betrothed, though she'd only met the man half a dozen times within the past five years. Her grandmother had influenced Alena's father to arrange the match, and honoring her wish, the betrothal was set once Alena reached the age of fifteen. Balen would have claimed her much sooner, but her father had been loath to let her go. His health in decline, he relied upon her more and more each day, it seemed. Alena's mother had long since passed away, and then her grandmother had died. Alena was the only family he had left, and she couldn't bear the thought of leaving him in the care of the servants.

"We'll see to your bags, my lady," the head of the guards said.

Timms opened both doors wide and stepped back. "Please, come inside and make yourself comfortable. Jackson can show your men where to place your bags."

A young man with bushy, black hair stepped forward, nodded in Alena's direction, and went outside to the coach.

Alena followed Timms, who led her through the grand entranceway and to a doorway on the right. She entered a large room with a pair of chairs and a settee placed before the hearth. Other chairs were positioned throughout the room, along with small tables bearing lit candles. The walls were lined with bookshelves containing hundreds of books.

"Please, be seated, and I will inform his lordship of your arrival."

Timms left the room, and Alena sat down before the hearth. Though the fire blazed with warmth, she felt a chill—from her recent ordeal with the wolves or the thought of facing Balen again, she wasn't sure.

It wasn't long before he came into the

room. "Alena?"

She got to her feet, ready with an apology. "Balen, please forgive my early arrival."

She took in the sight of him with a combination of relief and apprehension. He was dressed all in black, his tall black boots adding to his great height. His blond hair brushed his shoulders in stark contrast to his dark clothing.

He waved off her explanation and took both of her hands in his. "Not at all. I'm delighted." He peered into her eyes intently. "I have the feeling it was not the dire need to be by my side that has brought you here, however."

She looked down at her feet. "My father. He's had a stroke."

"I'm so sorry to hear that." He ran his thumbs over her knuckles, causing her pulse to quicken.

"I did not want to leave him. He is quite insensible. He cannot move, and he does not know who I am."

Balen urged her to retake her seat on the settee and sat down next to her. "How terrible."

"I know it's wrong for me to leave him this way. But I fear I had no choice." Her voice was barely a whisper. The past few days had been exhausting, and now that she had at last reached her destination, her fear and sadness pressed in on her.

"No choice?" There was a slight edge to his voice.

Alena wrung her hands and lifted her head to stare into eyes so dark they appeared black. "Another man seeks to make me his wife."

Anger flashed in his expression. "Who is this man?"

"Lord Rory Alden. His estate borders my father's land. And I fear…"

"You fear?"

"I fear he pursues me even now. He will not let me go."

Balen rose to his feet. His muscular strength and incredible height presented an awesome presence. "He will give you no more cause to fret, my love. I promise you."

Sweet words meant to give her reassurance sounded more like a brutal fact.

Alena shivered again.

CHAPTER 2

LORD OF THE HUNT

"Who is this man?" Tristan asked.

Alena had filled Balen in on several details before he settled her into her rooms. He'd then taken one of the secret passageways into the bowels of the castle. Tristan had been waiting for him, as Balen knew he would be.

"Lord Rory Alden. Hails from Elbrock Manor, the neighboring estate to Bradderly— Alena's father's estate. His family is newly come to the area." Balen paced back and forth before the huge hearth where a warm fire blazed. Both men held a glass of whiskey.

"He believes he has a claim to her?"

"He wishes it to be so. Apparently, he's given pursuit, chasing her across the miles, never letting up on his intent to overtake her."

"It's possible her father may not have opposed and perhaps even encouraged the match. He would not have to send his only child so far away then."

"She says Alden's been hanging around Bradderly since he moved in over a year ago. He is charming and gracious. Count Harford has been completely taken in."

"And how does Alena feel about him, or do I need to ask?" Tristan said. He drained his glass and reached for the bottle.

"She doesn't trust him. She said he makes her skin crawl, but she cannot pinpoint why."

"Sixth sense. We know all about that."

Balen snatched the whiskey bottle off the table and topped up his own drink. "He made his intention to court Alena clear to her father several months ago. Alena objected, of course, being already betrothed to me. But he is persistent. When Harford had a stroke, Alena feared Alden would take advantage of the opportunity, so she fled."

"And Alden gives pursuit," Tristan remarked with a scowl. "Let's give him a warm welcome, shall we?"

The two men contemplated each other in silence for a moment.

Balen set down his glass. "Are you ready? We have work to do."

Tristan nodded, his face grim. They both reached for a shovel and, without another word, climbed the stairs and headed out into the dark night.

"This is the place," Balen remarked when they came upon the roadway where the confrontation occurred between the wolves and Alena's guards.

The coachman's body was the first they moved off into the thick forest to bury.

Caleb was next. They both stared down at the body, now transformed into a naked man.

Balen sniffed the air, searching and deciphering the foreign scents.

"I didn't mean for this to happen," Tristan said. "You know how things can get in the heat of the battle."

"This was no battle," Balen reminded him. "It was pure sport. Entertainment to alleviate boredom."

"It's the bloody change. It takes over me, I feel like I have no control. Especially on nights like this."

They both stared up at the full moon.

After the men were buried, Balen and Tristan began the trek back to the castle. Balen was deep in thought. Seeing his two kinfolk transformed from the state of wolves back to men made him realize something he hadn't before.

For generations, the change had occurred, striking as soon as the victim reached the age of eighteen. There were rumors about how it all came to pass. Most agreed it was a curse placed upon the Cole family over two hundred years ago by a scorned woman rumored to have been a witch. All of those afflicted with the condition were related by blood, even remotely. Over the years, those relatives who'd heard the rumors about the Cole family arrived on the doorstep of the ancient holding, seeking sanctuary and comradery for their shared indisposition. Balen was wary to reveal the family secret to new arrivals, and only when he saw for himself the change come over the man — as it only affected the males of the bloodline — were they then welcomed into the pack.

The idea of stopping the transformation drove Balen to search endlessly for a cure. Many hours he spent below Terron Castle in his laboratory looking for the answer.

Now, he pondered the idea of death. With death, the wolf reverted back to man. What if that was the answer?

"I will greet Lady Alena in the morning," Tristan said as they came up before the kitchen door of Terron.

Balen cringed. "Please refrain from growling at my lady. She is of a delicate nature."

Tristan put his hand to his heart and grinned like a rogue. "Wouldn't dream of it. Good night, cousin."

Balen climbed atop the ancient battlements, surveying the dark land below, opting to not yet seek his bed. He inhaled deeply, searching for a scent. He'd never met Alden, but his keen sense of smell would detect a newcomer easily. The trace of Alena's guard was heavy on the air. He didn't know if Alden's scent was mingled with the others. Balen knew he must be close.

The fear in Alena's voice and expression told him this was no trifling matter. Alden meant to have her. Balen was just as determined that he would not.

The problem he faced was how to remove the threat. It would be easy enough to hunt the man down and blame his demise on a wolf attack. But he didn't need a mass hunting party arriving, attempting to eliminate the pack. The death of a hired coachman was one thing. The death of a lord would be taken more seriously.

Balen and his pack were the only

anomaly in the area and quite hidden at that. He preferred things to stay that way. It was true that Tristan and the others could get a little wild now and again. It wasn't unheard of to have nearby farmers arrive at his doorstep with a grievance of livestock being killed, unaware they were speaking to the overlord of the pack. Tristan and some of the others had a wild streak to them, which Balen had tried over the years — most unsuccessfully — to curb.

Tonight, things had gone too far. Two members of his pack had been senselessly killed. The young black had been a member for only a few months, but Balen and Caleb had been close for years.

Restless, Balen left the battlements and wove through the labyrinth of hidden passageways, finding himself in Alena's bedroom. Staring down upon her, curled up on her side, blankets pulled up to her chin, he felt a surge of protectiveness.

She was so innocent. And she knew nothing of the curse.

If he prevailed in finding a cure, she never would.

* * * *

Alena sensed a presence.

She kept her breathing slow and even and her body still, giving the impression she slept. All she saw through the slits of her eyes were shadows — given off by the crackling flames in the hearth, or something else, she knew not which. Her skin did not prickle in warning, so she felt no danger. The deep breaths she heard were unmistakable, and the scent... Ah, now she recognized it, for it lingered over the entire place, so she did not at first discern it. But now it was so strong — Balen.

How had he come to be at the foot of her bed? She'd not heard the heavy door to her room swing open. He must have a secret entrance. The window was open, but he could hardly have come through there.

Or had he?

Ever since she'd been a child at her grandmother's knee, she'd heard rumors about the Cole family's history. Stories about a curse and a witch. And something about packs of wolves. Come to think of it, Rory had even relayed some of these tales to her and her father. No doubt, hoping to cast a poor light upon her betrothed.

Alena had to admit the rumors only added to the intrigue and mystery of Balen Cole and Terron Castle. Now that she was here, she felt strangely content. Fear for her father was still prominent in her mind, however, and at the soonest opportunity, she hoped to convince Balen to allow her father to come here to join them. Yet, for the first time in days, she didn't fear that Rory would come upon her and snatch her away. Everything about that man screamed 'danger.'

Light footsteps sounded, and Alena heard a scratching noise, which sounded like a panel being moved. The hidden passageway. She soon sensed she was alone once more. After a few minutes, she pushed the blankets back and crept from her bed. She moved toward the place where she'd heard the sound. It took a while, but she discovered the secret door and how to access it from her side. Satisfied, she crossed the room to the large window. The shutters lay open, allowing in the cool, fresh night air.

She looked at the bedroom door to see that it remained latched. Only then did she loosen the ties on her nightgown and let it slip off to pool at her feet. Slowly, she raised her arms into the air, letting the gentle breeze blow over her bare skin.

Seconds later, the change came upon her.

She rose up into the air on great, powerful, snowy white wings and soared through the window into the dark night.

* * * *

The next morning, Alena sat for breakfast at the table with Balen. He noted the smudges beneath her eyes and figured she'd not passed a restful night.

"You have a beautiful home," Alena said. She sipped at her second cup of coffee.

"Thank you. Once we've finished, I'll take you on a tour of the castle and the grounds."

"Is it true Terron is three hundred years old?"

Balen nodded. "Yes, it's been in my family for generations. It's not a great castle by any means, but it's home."

After breakfast, Balen took her on a grand tour, eulogizing the history of the Cole family. He wondered, as he stared at her curious gaze, what rumors she'd heard about him and of Terron. He knew the talk of curses and wild beasts stretched out farther than the small surrounding hamlets. Whether the stories reached all the way to Alena's former home, he couldn't say.

The last place Balen brought her was

atop the battlements. They stared out across the land. "The forest stretches for miles in every direction," he said. "Over there is the town of Mardow. It's very old, over a hundred years." He pointed in that direction.

Alena nodded.

Balen took in her searching gaze and thought she was most likely scanning the area for signs of Alden. He tilted his head back and breathed deeply, searching for a new scent.

"We can take the horses out if you're not too tired," Balen offered.

She smiled. "I'd like that. Have we seen all of the castle then? What about below? Is that where you keep the deep, dark dungeon?"

Balen tensed. "Long ago, there were a couple of prison cells. Now it's mainly used for storage." The last thing he wanted was for Alena to go below and see the laboratory he had set up. "Perhaps we should discuss our wedding?"

* * * *

Hours later, they reined in their heavily breathing horses. Balen was pleased to learn his betrothed was an accomplished rider. He'd loved racing her through the meadow and then wandering the endless forest trails before racing back through the meadow again.

He hadn't returned to the castle. Instead, he'd led them to a private glen beside a small pond he enjoyed swimming in. He produced a basket from behind one of the broad trees and a large, soft quilt. He laid it on the grassy bank while the horses took their ease. Alena sat down upon the blanket.

"You've done some planning, I see," she said.

Together, they emptied the basket. After lunch, they finished off a bottle of wine.

"I would like my father to be here for our wedding," Alena said. Upon their ride, they'd discussed marrying as soon as possible.

"Is he fit to travel?" Balen asked. He was anxious to marry Alena, not only to secure her safety, but too, he wanted her in his bed.

She shrugged. "I'm not certain. I do hope he will be in condition to soon." She packed up the empty dishes and put the basket aside. She laid back and stared up at the blue sky.

"You are tired," Balen noted. He shifted, feeling his prick harden at the sight of his betrothed laying down beside him.

When she smiled at him and shook her head in denial, he bent and kissed her on the lips. He was surprised when her hand came up against his chest to caress him. The kiss deepened, and the tips of their tongues met and danced.

Balen pulled away. "We should not," he said, making to rise. He was only too aware of their location. Though private, anyone could interrupt them at any moment.

Alena reached out to take his arm. "You wish to wait until we're wed?"

He nodded once and stared at her hand, amazed at the heat of her touch.

"Truly? I had thought..." Her voice trailed off, but he couldn't miss the note of regret.

He settled back down beside her. "What would you like, my love?" he asked.

Her tongue flicked out to moisten her lower lip. "I want you, my lord."

"You do not wish to wait?"

She shook her head and reached for him. He kissed her again. When their tongues met, he did not pull away but delved deeper. Her hands moved to his shirt, and swiftly, he removed his clothing before helping to remove hers.

He stared down at her naked body and marveled over her beauty. He'd imagined her like this, laying naked before him. His dreams were but a pale comparison to reality. Large, full breasts tipped with rosy pink nipples taunted him. Her waist was narrow, and her hips flared out seductively. Long legs enticed his eyes to travel to where her thighs met to conceal her secret delights.

He didn't know where to begin.

* * * *

Alena watched Balen, intently aware of his hot gaze sliding over every inch of her body. Being outside, surrounded by nature, with the threat of discovery, only added to her excitement. She'd imagined this moment, but not like this. Instead, she'd given herself to Balen behind a locked door, in the comfort of a bed.

A soft, warm breeze caressed her naked flesh. Bird songs serenaded them. Tall, sturdy trees stood sentry.

This was far better.

The sight of his naked body was beautiful. Muscle accented his broad chest and flowed throughout his powerful arms and legs. She smiled at the sight of his huge feet, but her breath froze as her gaze traveled upward to his prick. Standing erect, its massive size made her eyes widen in alarm. Tentatively, she reached out to take it in her hand. Smooth silk covered his long, hard length. She'd never seen a man's prick before. His was surely the most glorious of all. She stroked her hand up and down, prompting grunts of approval.

"Do I please you, my lord?"

He nodded and reached out with greedy hands for her breasts. He dipped his head to fasten his mouth on her nipple, tugging at it teasingly, making her back arch up in delight. Alena reveled in the sensation and noted the instant changes in her body. Her breath came in quick little pants. Her skin grew hot and tingly. Yearning gnawed in her belly, and that hidden place between her thighs making her ache for him. She lifted a hand to delve deep in his thick, blond tresses.

His fingers trailed down her belly and between her legs, urging her thighs to part. As he laved her other nipple, his finger dipped inside her, eliciting a gasp. Never could she have imagined the intensity his touch created in her body. She concentrated on his mouth and then on his finger, soon joined by another, probing deep inside her. Her head rolled from side to side.

He pulled his fingers free and moved overtop of her, between her legs, guiding the tip of his prick to her passage.

"There will be pain," he warned gently.

"I know." She could bear anything so long as he put an end to her torment.

Slowly, he entered her, pushing deep inside. He breached her maidenhead and stilled, waiting for her to relax. The discomfort passed, quickly replaced by desire. She lifted her legs and ran her hands down his back to urge him on. He withdrew and surged forward, stroking her again and again, each plunge growing swifter. Her hands grabbed his ass and squeezed, feeling his muscles strain. She moved her hips, matching his rhythm.

"My lord…" Her nails dug into his skin. She wanted—needed—something but knew not what.

Balen took her hands and held them over her head, no doubt feeling the sting of the scratches she'd raked down his back. He kissed her hard, his tongue darting into her mouth, matching the tempo of his strokes.

"Come for me," he said.

Alena gripped his hands tight and tensed as her passion built and built until finally shattering. She cried out, and seconds later, Balen stilled and hollered his own release.

Sweaty and sated, the pair held each other close.

* * * *

That night, beneath Terron Castle, Balen stood before a table with Tristan at his side. From a saddlebag, he pulled out a cloth, set it on the table, and unwrapped a dark green plant topped by a purple flower.

"Out on a ride today with Alena, I was able to gather this." He felt a heat in his groin at the thought of how they'd spent the rest of the afternoon.

"Wolfsbane?" Tristan recoiled.

Balen regarded him grimly. "Yes. And before you ask, I know what it's capable of."

"So the question is, what do you plan to do with it? Does this have anything to do with Alden?"

"It's not just the problem of his presence, which I detected today. He's close. It's also to do with our pack and ending the curse."

Tristan stared at him. "The curse? You think to end it with this?" He gestured to the deadly plant.

"It's risky, but if we die as a wolf, we revert back to a man. There is an antidote."

Tristan stared at him incredulously.

"And you believe if we kill the wolf, we'll end the curse. You're willing to risk death for it?"

"And to save Alena," Balen confirmed. The only way to end the threat Alden posed to Alena was to kill him or at least send a brutal message. Either way, it must be done as the wolf. As a man, he dared not risk killing or even physically threatening Alden for fear of being prosecuted and leaving Alena once more vulnerable. Getting rid of Alden, by way of the wolf, would set his pack up for being hunted and killed. But if there were no wolves to find…

He wrapped up the wolfsbane, careful not to touch it with his bare hands, and set it aside. The shelves near the table held many small vials, mortars, pestles, and several dried plants and herbs. Balen set out what he needed and went to work.

* * * *

Alena knew that Balen was up to something. In the form of a snowy white owl, she perched outside the tiny window used for ventilation from the bowels of Terron Castle. From here, she easily overheard Balen's dangerous plan. For her, he would attempt to end the curse of the wolf. Hearing his and Tristan's conversation, it was obvious to concede that the rumors about the Cole bloodline were true.

She'd hoped that Balen was indeed, such as she, an anomaly. But if he looked upon his metamorphosis as a curse, then what would he do when he ultimately discovered what she was? Would he, perchance, want to risk his 'cure' on her as well? The thought disturbed her. He may be willing to do anything to cast off his alternate identity, to become a normal human being, whereas she rejoiced in hers. To experience the freedom and thrill of flying through the night sky wasn't something she was eager to relinquish.

Today, she and Balen had discussed their wedding. Though they'd not yet set an exact date, they'd been in agreement to do the deed soon. She'd relayed her wish to have her father present here on that day if he recovered enough to make it a reality. Balen agreed to wait, but he was pragmatic. If her father showed no signs of recovery before All Hallows' Eve, the next full moon, then they would marry despite his absence. Alena couldn't fault his plan. They both knew the threat Rory presented. She had no doubt the rogue would find a way to lure her back home and attempt to accost her on the road unless he grew restless and set upon her sooner.

He was near. Her senses tingled, and the breeze brought faint trails of his scent to her. Balen had sensed him as well. No doubt it being the reason why he worked even now to prevent him from stealing her away.

She flew off into the darkness and ascended over the land which was to be her home. Soaring near and far, high and low, she searched the land for her nemesis. She combed through the small town, the forests, and the fields before she finally gained success. A tiny campfire alerted her to the band of men tucked deep among the thick trees half a league from Terron.

Silently, she came to rest high atop a tree limb to look down upon them. The soft snores and occasional snorts confirmed they were asleep. From the array of weapons and the rough appearance of Rory's cohorts, Alena feared he was deep into this escapade. She couldn't understand the tenacity of the man. She'd made it perfectly clear she had no wish to be with him. Why couldn't he take no for an answer? Perhaps it wasn't only her he coveted? Maybe it was her father's land and estate he desired as well? Whatever it was, he did not appear to be a man to accept defeat gracefully. The only way to end this dilemma would be to scare him off. If that didn't work, they would have to do whatever it took to stop him.

Even if it meant his death.

CHAPTER 3
LORD OF THE HUNT

The next morning at breakfast, Alena couldn't mistake the glint in Balen's eyes. The smile he shared with her revealed he'd enjoyed yesterday's afternoon romp and no doubt desired an encore. Judging by the smudges beneath his eyes, it appeared it'd been his turn to spend a restless night. She wondered how long he had worked on his antidote. She assumed it was what had kept him in the castle cellar so late.

As for herself, she'd returned to her open window shortly after discovering the band of wretches in the forest. Obviously, Balen was aware of their close proximity. Knowing the drastic measures he was prepared to take to protect her and his pack, she feared she must change her plans. She'd had every intention of revealing her true nature to her betrothed, but she'd also hoped to have more time. Necessity would force her revelation to come sooner rather than later. She was certain that together, combining their skills, they could deal with Rory without risking Balen's life or endangering the pack.

"Sleep well, my love?" He brushed a kiss across her lips before sitting down.

"Yes, thank you. You?"

He shrugged.

"Does something trouble you?" she ventured.

"Nothing for you to worry about," he assured her.

"I thought we might ride out today?" She knew he would not mistake the innuendo she presented. The thought of him taking her outside again, surrounded by the forest, made her squirm with excitement.

He arched an eyebrow and leered suggestively. "Another picnic, perhaps?"

She nodded conspiratorially.

When he took her hand beneath the table, Alena was tempted to press it against the juncture of her thighs. Her boldness startled her. Only yesterday, she'd been an untried virgin. Although, she knew it was desire that had kept her up many a sleepless night in the past, especially after a visit to their home from the mysterious and handsome Lord Cole.

After breakfast they went their separate ways; Alena to her rooms and Balen to the castle cellar to continue his work. Around noon, the pair met up in the barn as planned. She noted that this time, he had a picnic basket and blanket. So he planned to head right to their private spot and forgo a long ride. Good. She was more than ready for him. Although, after he made sweet love to her, she planned to expose herself to him even more intimately.

Should it prove to be her downfall, she knew not. Showing her true self to him may set his heart as hers forever or turn it completely to stone. She prayed it was the former.

* * * *

Balen brimmed with eagerness as they guided their mounts toward the glen by the pond. The place where he and Alena had made love yesterday. And where they planned to do it again today. Her passion had surprised and pleased him greatly. He knew they would be well matched as mates.

They dismounted, and he saw to the horses while Alena set out the blanket.

"Are you very hungry?" she asked.

By the predatory look she wore, now

leaning back upon her hands, legs out before her, he got the impression she was as anxious as him.

"This is my fault," he said, followed by a dramatic sigh.

Her brow furrowed in puzzlement. "What is?"

"One afternoon spent in my arms, and I've turned you into a brazen lover."

Her face lowered, and he worried he'd embarrassed her. But she met his gaze and smiled seductively.

"I find I cannot help myself." To prove her point, she stood up and began to slowly remove her dress.

His clothing came off more quickly.

Taking her in his arms, he lowered them to the blanket. He kissed her passionately, running his thumbs over her hardened nipples. Kisses trailed down her neck and chest and lower to her belly.

Alena entangled her fingers in his hair while he roamed even lower. His breath came out in hot pants as his tongue flicked against her other hard nub. He suckled, hearing her gasp, and felt her fingers tighten and her hips lift in greeting. He eased two fingers inside of her and then another, teasing her clit all the while.

When he shifted to position himself to claim her, she surprised him by urging him onto his back. She rained slow, seductive kisses on his chest, working her way lower, just as he had done to her. He startled, feeling her warm breath against his prick. She took him in her hand and began to stroke the long length of him. He nearly came undone when she put her mouth on him. Her tongue and lips caressed his shaft while she fondled his balls.

"My love," he moaned.

When he feared he would lose himself completely, he moved her onto her hands and knees before him. He admired the fine shape of her from this angle, head bowed, rear end up in the air, awaiting his attention. He ran his hands down her soft skin, over her ass, and between her legs, opening them wide. Hand on his prick, he guided it into place. As he eased forward, she looked back at him through a tangle of blonde curls and smiled.

Her look turned to one of surprise as he sank into her depth and began to move with slow, deliberate strokes. Gasps and low moans escaped her lips. She urged him on, pleading with him to go faster. He complied. Her breasts swayed, and he reached out to grasp them in his hands.

After several minutes, she dropped her head lower, and he took hold of her hips once more. His thrusts grew faster and faster. Together, they reached their peak, crying out in ecstasy before collapsing on the blanket.

They took time to share the picnic lunch and a bottle of wine, then resumed their lovemaking until dark shadows began to creep across the sky. The chill in the air alerted Balen to the late hour. They'd lost all track of time. Throughout the afternoon Alena had attempted to tell him something. He'd been so overcome with desire that he'd distracted her shamelessly. Now, he wondered what had been on her mind.

He kissed her to wake her from slumber. "Dearest, it's late. We should head back," he said with regret.

As they finished dressing, Balen's horse tossed its head and snorted. It used its front hoof to paw at the ground in agitation.

"What is it, boy?" He went over to calm the huge horse and heard a rustling in the forest. He cursed. His senses had been compromised by his lust. Quickly, he set his mount loose and smacked its bottom. "Run home!" he said.

Alena hurried over to him. "What is it? What's wrong?"

He grasped her around the waist and lifted her onto her horse. "Go back to the castle. Now," he said without explanation. He smacked her horse's rump, making her grasp the reins tight when it bolted toward Terron.

Balen stood alone in the clearing and waited, his senses quickly becoming fine-tuned and alert for danger.

Moments later, Lord Alden emerged from the forest. Everything about the man struck Balen as menacing. He could well understand Alena's repulsion for him. He was a large man, only an inch or so shorter than Balen's six four and almost as broad. His hair was brown, worn in tight curls to his collar. His eyes were a cold blue.

He came up before Balen and frowned. "Where is Alena? What have you done to her?"

Balen scowled at his familiar use of her name. "My betrothed has returned to Terron Castle. Though her whereabouts are no concern of yours."

"Of course, it concerns me. It is me that Alena loves. Not you. She only came here to break off your betrothal agreement. She said she owed it to you to do so in person and alone. I warned her you would take advantage of the situation." His gaze raked over the messed up blanket, and he scowled.

Balen took an intimidating step forward. "That is not what Alena tells me."

Alden smirked. "She was only to tell you that she no longer wishes to be wed. She was not about to admit she loves someone else. She fears you too greatly."

"She has no fear of me," Balen stated.

"No? Maybe not of you, perhaps. But what of your dark secrets? Yours and those of your bloodline?"

Balen knew that rumors abounded about the legend of the curse on his family. If there'd been any with proof against them, it would have surfaced by now. He laughed. "So you would believe stories told to you as a boy to keep you in your bed at night?"

"Not stories. I've seen your kind with my own eyes."

"Liar!"

Alden grinned, seeing he'd struck a nerve. "One night, when I was just a lad, my family traveled through this area. We were attacked—by wolves. When my father left the coach to aid the guards, he was set upon and killed. Our coach was ripped into. My mother and I were able to flee with help from the last guard before he was killed. We fled into the woods and hid. Much later, after my mother fell into a fitful slumber, I slipped away. I came upon the scene of carnage. My father, his throat torn, the guards, all dead. I heard a gasping sound and followed it. There, I saw a wolf brought down with a pike still sticking from its chest. I crept closer, wanting to kill the beast for the devastation it'd wrought. Before my eyes, the wolf, as it died, changed into a man."

Balen shrugged as though not concerned. "Fanciful imaginings of a distraught child." Years later, he'd heard this story from his own father, the pack leader at the time. It was told to him as a warning to heed. His father had not mentioned the boy.

"Your kind took my father from me. Now, I intend to take someone that you love. Do not think to stop me or I will have you face so much scrutiny you will never escape being discovered. It is my wish to drive you and your cursed kind off the face of this earth. However, I will show mercy and leave you in peace. So long as I have Alena."

"I will not barter her for your silence. You have no proof. Only a fabricated tale," Balen scoffed. He wasn't sure what to do. If he killed Alden, he would have the authorities down on his head.

Alden moved back and pulled a knife from his jacket. "Come out," he cried. Three rough-looking men appeared from the forest and spaced out to surround Balen. Each of them held a large knife. "One way or another, I will have her."

"You would attack me, lord of this land, and hope to get away with it?"

Alden smiled wickedly. "No one knows of my presence here. By the time your body is discovered, Alena will be my wife and will not dare speak against me."

White-hot rage settled over Balen. One of the men positioned himself before Balen's cloak, which lay on the ground, and held his own weapon. Unarmed, he could not hope to survive the attack of four men. If he perished, Alena would be at Alden's mercy.

Seeing no choice, he forced the transformation to come upon him, knowing he had better odds as the wolf. Soon, he faced his enemy, his clothing shredded around him. He could not allow Alena to be taken. He would ensure her safety, even if it meant his death.

He threw his head back and howled.

* * * *

Alena's horse traveled only a short distance before she gained control of it and reined it to a halt. She dismounted and sent it on to the stables before racing back in Balen's direction. As she neared, she heard the howl of a wolf. Fearing the worst, she tore at her clothing and quickly transformed into an owl, and soared into the darkening sky.

Overtop the clearing where scant hours ago she'd been basking in Balen's arms, a terrible scene greeted her. Four men, knives glinting in the dying light, surrounded a lone silver wolf. As they advanced upon the animal, she recognized them as Rory and his band of thugs.

As she dove, she saw the wolf lunge. She knew it was Balen, the wolf who had saved her the other night. He'd risked his life for her then, just as she knew he did now. Softly, she came to land upon the ground just out of sight at the edge of the glen. She changed back into human form, and while the men were distracted, she reached out to snatch Balen's cloak. Swinging it around her naked form, she felt the weight of the weapon in the inner pocket. Pulling the knife free, she inched around the area until she came upon Rory. Silently, she stalked up behind him and poked the tip of the blade against his neck.

"Call off your men," she hissed.

He spun around so quickly that he caught her off-guard. She flung to the ground but rose carefully, the blade still grasped in her hand.

"You heard me," she said, noting he held his own knife in his grip.

"Alena! Thank God you're safe," he said.

Her gaze flashed between him and the melee going on. No one else took note of her — yet. "Of course I'm safe, you idiot. Now call off your men."

"I have come to save you." He appeared taken off-guard by her harsh tone.

A scream sounded as the silver wolf clamped his teeth on one of the men's arms, stripping him of his weapon. The man shook free and ran off, holding his bloody limb.

"Save me? From my betrothed?" she snapped.

"Yes, that devil! He's not what he appears to be, dearest."

Alena cringed at his endearment. "I

know exactly what he is."

"He's a wolf!"

"And you're a chicken!"

He recoiled at her words. "What say you?"

She took a step closer to him. "I say you are a chicken! You gathered those brutes to fight one unarmed man."

He bit his lip for a moment, thinking. "I could take no chances with your safety. You see what he is." Rory waved his knife, indicating the wolf, who was now dispatching his second assailant, sending him fleeing into the woods.

"I'm here to even the odds."

He slipped the blade into the pocket of his cloak and held up his hands. "You are safe now, I assure you. Put the knife away, Alena."

"You mistake me, sir. I have not come to turn the odds more in your favor. I side with my betrothed."

"Then you are a fool," he snarled.

He rushed forward, surprising her. They struggled. Rory, being so much larger and stronger, soon wrested the knife from her. Fearful, Alena's gaze flashed to Balen.

As though sensing her presence, the wolf paused in his pursuit of his last assailant. The moment he looked at her, Alena threw off the cloak and changed into an owl. She flapped her wings and began to lift up into the air. Just as she made to fly away, one of her sharp talons snagged upon the cloak. Weighted down, she could not escape.

Rory's face portrayed his shock and rage at seeing her transformation. He raised the knife and aimed it at her breast. "Evil, vile freak of nature!" he spat.

Trapped, Alena frantically tried to break free. Rory halted her attempt, stomping his foot upon the heavy fabric.

"You must die!" he cried.

Just as Rory swung his arm, Balen leaped for his throat. Alena watched in horror as the pair fell to the ground. Swiftly, she landed and returned to human form.

"Balen!" She threw the cloak over her shoulders and crouched beside the wolf. She laid her hands upon his soft, silver coat. Beneath him lay Rory's still form.

Howls and barks sounded, growing louder, and soon, dozens of wolves burst into the glen. A lone rider appeared among the animals and reined in steps from Alena.

"Tristan!" she gasped, rising to her feet.

"Balen was attacked by Lord Alden and his men. Alden lies here beneath him. The others have fled."

He leapt from the horse. "Go! Scour the woods!" he hollered at the wolves who were pacing restlessly. The pack took off into the forest to hunt.

"He is so still. I am afraid," Alena said.

Tristan lifted Balen and moved him aside. Rory's throat was bloodied, and it was clear to see he no longer lived.

"No!" Alena cried, seeing the dagger buried in the wolf's chest.

Tristan dropped to his knees and sunk his hands deep into the thick fur. "I can feel a heartbeat, but it's faint."

Before their eyes, Balen transformed into a man. The knife came free and fell to his side. Alena feared that the wolf had died. She knelt and placed her hands on Balen's bare chest and sobbed. "He fought for me. He died for me!"

Tristan reached out and laid his hand on hers, his own eyes filling with tears.

Off in the distance, howls and mad barking soon turned to shouts of men. Moments later, many of them appeared in the clearing, covering their nakedness with branches of leaves or their hands.

"We have changed!" one of them declared. "All of us. Something has happened."

Silently, the men gathered around their lord, who lay near dead.

"He must have broken the curse," Tristan stated, no joy in his voice.

Alena stared at Balen in despair as his eyes fluttered open.

"My love," he gasped. "You are safe?"

She nodded. "Yes, dearest. Thanks to you."

Balen turned his gaze to Tristan. "Watch over her, cousin."

Tristan nodded and grasped his lord's hand.

"I cannot let you go," Alena cried. "I love you. You must live."

A sudden heat overcame her. She stared at her hands, pressing against the bloodied wound in Balen's chest. A glowing, white light appeared and encompassed Balen's body, lifting him inches above the ground. It shimmered brightly and then faded away as his body lowered.

Miraculously, before their eyes, Balen's wound began to heal. Soon, his chest rose and fell with deep, strong breaths.

Alena and Tristan, and the men circling them, moved back with a start when Balen suddenly sat up.

"What magic is this?" Tristan cried, his eyes wide with disbelief.

Balen ran his hands over his chest in awe and blinked rapidly. The men cheered, and Alena embraced him.

"You have broken the curse with your love," she said, suddenly recalling the ancient tale her grandmother had told her.

"What do you mean, Alena?" Balen asked.

"When I was a young girl, my grandmother told me a story about a curse placed long ago on a man who had broken a woman's heart. That woman was my ancestor, my grandmother said." She recited, *"And until such a time that a descendant from that cursed man enacts a selfless deed of love for someone from my bloodline, the curse shall stand."*

With Tristan's help, Balen rose to his feet. Alena stood and pulled the cape tighter around her, feeling the rapt attention from all the men in the clearing.

Balen took her hand. "Are you saying

you are descended from the woman who placed the curse of the wolf upon my family?"

She nodded. "I believe I am. Although, I must admit I never gave much belief to the tale. I'm surprised I remembered it now."

"So my saving you broke the curse?"

"Yes. It took the life of the wolf but not yours." She felt a tear slip down her cheek. Balen reached out and brushed it away gently with his hand.

Tristan removed his cloak and passed it to Balen. "I will leave the horse for you. Come, you naked fools," he said with a laugh to the men. "Let us give our lord and his lady some privacy. I will return later and bury the wretch." He put his hand on Balen's shoulder for a moment and gave Alena a wink. Then he turned and strode toward the woods and Terron Castle with the others.

Alena stared at Balen in silence, contemplating her next words.

"I saw…" Balen began.

"You saw me change," Alena said.

"Yes. What a wonder! I never imagined such a beautiful sight."

Alena smiled with relief. "I wanted to tell you, but I was afraid."

He laughed. "I wanted to tell you, as well, about the wolf. But I, too, was afraid."

She took his hand. "There was another part of the tale my grandmother told me. She said when the two lovers conquered the curse, they would forever soar together."

"What do you think that means?" Balen asked.

Alena stepped back and dropped the cloak. "Let us see, my love. Follow me."

She changed into a snowy white owl and flew off, circling the man she loved.

Balen stilled for only a moment, then threw off his cloak and concentrated. Seconds later, he turned into a huge, silver owl. He stretched out his massive wings, acquainting himself with the sensation. Soon, he lifted up to take flight.

Together, the pair soared off into the dark night sky, forever united in their love.

Step in Time

CHAPTER 1

STEP IN TIME

It was a moment in time — a blip, some would call it. A fluke. A random peek at the unexplained. Most unusual and never glimpsed before or again. But I've seen it, felt it, and lived it. And I alone caused it to come about. Some may call it chance. I call it destiny.

My name is Starr. And this is my story.

I write this tale of mine here, where it all began, at Stonehenge. Set off across the field, far from the allure of the stones, I sit. And remember.

Stonehenge had always been a place of intrigue for me. Since I was a little girl and first saw a picture of the mysterious standing stones on the Salisbury Plains, I knew I had to come. I grew up in a tiny, dank apartment in downtown Toronto with my mother. Having me on her own at age forty made her seem ancient to me. I was grateful for her love. I believe it was that love that made her hold on to life despite her ever-present illness. At least until I reached the age of eighteen, safe from the system. I was an adult, could do as I pleased, and what I longed to do was dance.

Dancing was something I'd dreamed of doing for as long as I could remember. When I was twelve my mother encouraged me to audition for a little theater group around the corner from our apartment. They saw potential in the thin, shy, wide-eyed girl with blonde hair much too long. They took me in, nurtured me, and made me one of them. Taught me to hone my skill. To evolve from someone who merely dances well into someone who becomes one with dance. I danced freestyle, loving the way I could turn several steps I'd mastered into a dance that was mine alone.

The theater was a second home to me. Every evening, weekend, and holiday, I was there. Dancing was my escape. My life. My mentor and instructor, Savannah, said that when I danced, I went away somewhere. A place where nothing could touch me. Savannah said I was mystique, hypnotizing. I grabbed her heart with my movements so compellingly that she said she could feel her heartbeat, and my steps become one. I could feel what she could see.

Once I graduated from high school, I danced full-time. I had no one waiting for me at home, so I stayed at the theater late every night, rehearsing and putting on performances with the others. My dedication paid off. I miserly scrimped and saved. Two years it took me to have enough money to finally visit England. And Stonehenge. I knew that it would somehow change my life forever. I just didn't realize how much. I came alone and stayed at a bed-and-breakfast close by, thumbed a ride in the late afternoon, and waited.

"Is this not the most amazing thing you've ever seen?"

I started for a moment, breaking from my concentration, to focus on the young man who'd wandered up beside me.

"Ah, yes. Amazing." The music in my head was almost drowning out the sounds of the others around me. I tried to attune my attention to the man who continued to speak while gazing in awe at the colossal stones around us.

"I've waited a long time to come here to see this," he told me, leaning close and whispering the words conspiratorially.

I moved back, pretending to get a better

view of the large stone before me. Not that I wished to be rude, but the moment was mine to seize alone. I, too, had come a long way to see these stones, waiting forever, it felt like, to finally be standing right where I was.

Soon, clouds reached across the evening sky like greedy fingers covering up the light. Mingling crowds thinned. People set off across the fields to their cars and tour buses waiting to whisk them back to civilization. I patiently remained until I stood alone before Stonehenge. The name alone set my imagination alight. It took everything inside of me to still my body despite the tempting melody playing in my head.

At long last, when every car had driven away, I slipped over the barrier and walked forward to lay my hand against a smooth, cool stone. A vibration tingled in my fingers, emanating, I'm certain, from the stone itself. Others had reported this sensation as well, so I knew it wasn't my fanciful mind. The song in my head seemed in tune with the vibration, as though they were one, finally coming together.

Though the land around me grew darker each moment, the light of the full moon climbing up in the sky cast an eerie glow. I sat and leaned back against the stone, removing my shoes and waiting barefoot until the moonlight shone directly on Stonehenge, just as the ancient people ordained. Once that happened, I stood, removed my long, thin sweater, and brushed off my silvery dress, which reached just below my knees. I walked to the center of the stones. The music in my head was achingly intent. It would not be denied.

I raised my hands up over my head and arched my left foot, anxious to begin. I closed my eyes and let the music overtake my body. Slowly, at first, I moved, allowing myself to become one with the melody. I turned and bent forward, brushing my fingertips upon the soft grass, stretching my right leg out and up, tilting toward the sky. I remained still for only a moment, taking my strength from the land around me. Then I began to move. Faster and faster. My dress swirled and lifted, caressing my thighs as I spun.

I'd spent my time here studying the stones. They were imprinted in my memory, and though I danced around them, touching them gently now and then, I did not fear spinning into one of them. I'd waited far too long for this opportunity. Long had I dreamed of dancing here. Alone. And yet, strangely not. It was as though I danced through time, my heart and soul mingling with those who had been here before me. Centuries past, generations and generations of people. Those who were curious and in awe. And farther back to those who had known the secrets.

Time stood still while I danced. It had no choice. It watched me move with precision, rapture. To move time would hurry my steps and cease them sooner. And so I danced for time. I envisioned *him* as a lover. I made love as only a dancer could — with exquisite movement meant to steal one's breath, to race a heart. I wanted, needed, to make it mine.

Only exhaustion made me finally slow my pace and lower my arms. I waited a moment and then opened my eyes. Though the night was dark, the moon's glow was still bright. It lit upon the formations around me, but as my eyes focused and then widened in wonder, I saw that instead of stone surrounding me, it was wood. Wooden posts, to be exact. Spread out in a circle around the perimeter of the slight incline. The posts stood firm and defiant, as though challenging time to topple them over as it had the sturdy stones. I closed my eyes tight and opened them again, so sure, I must be mistaken in what I saw. But no, when I looked again, the posts remained.

"Are you kidding me?" I said aloud, my fear and confusion making me voice my dismay.

My gaze swept the landscape, and I could not find comfort in its familiarity, for though it appeared almost the same, it too was different. I looked to where I'd left my shoes and sweater and noticed they were gone.

"What the hell?" My voice sounded strange, frightened, yet it gave me comfort to hear my words spoken aloud. I wandered around the posts, placing my hands upon one, just as I had the stone. It hummed. "Strange."

Perhaps it was this place that caused the vibration? I'd read that throughout the years, it had been described as alive with energy.

A sudden snap caught my attention, causing me to spin around. "Who's there?"

A man stepped forward from behind one of the tall posts across from me. I immediately became alarmed when he didn't speak, he just stood staring as I stared back. The first thing I noticed was his great size. I knew if he came closer, he would tower over me. His hair was remarkable, long, brushing his shoulders, and as golden as mine. The moonlight shone upon his broad, almost bare, leather-vested chest. His long, muscular legs were encased in what appeared to be pants made from the hide of an animal. Tall boots, seemingly of fur and thick hide, came up almost to his knees. The thing that struck me most was the look on his face, a combination of admiration and fear.

I held up my hand before me as though the gesture would keep him at bay. When he took a step closer, I retreated.

"Wait," came his deep voice.

"Don't come any closer."

We stared at each other in silence.

"My name is Slane," he said at last. His look was expectant, as though waiting for me to tell him mine.

"I'm Starr." I detected a slight lilt to his voice that I couldn't quite place. At least I could understand him.

"Where did you come from?" He swept his gaze around as though looking for the answer.

That was the million-dollar question. I knew instinctively that I was no longer where I'd been several minutes ago. Not only were my surroundings different, but the air seemed fresher, untainted. The matter presenting itself now, I believe, was *when* was I? Judging by the clothes Slane had on and the wooden posts around us, I was pretty certain I'd traveled back in time. Somehow, someway, as crazy as it seemed, at this moment, it became entirely possible.

I calculated quickly in my mind about what I remembered of Stonehenge. It was built on and off throughout the millenniums, beginning about five thousand years ago. So I'd gone at least that far. *Great.*

Slane was waiting for my answer. I had to tell him something without freaking him out. "I have no idea." *Think, think, think!*

"She is from the heavens." That voice came from behind me, not from Slane.

I spun around and saw a huge, incredibly handsome man similarly dressed to Slane coming toward us. In contrast to Slane's golden beauty, this man was dark. Bronze skin, shoulder-length black hair. His speech was different as well. His accent thicker. I could understand him but had to listen carefully.

I focused on the club he held threateningly in his hands. I whipped my head back to Slane and noticed something I hadn't before. Balanced in his left hand, he held a weapon as well. A spear resting against his thigh. As I watched, he lifted the weapon and posed battle-ready, the look on his face turning dark.

Back and forth, I darted my gaze, watching both men, worried they would pounce while I stood precariously between them. An obvious tension filled the air as they regarded each other with lethal glares and tight grips on their weapons.

There has to be something said about the irony of timing. I had magically appeared in this place, not coming upon an innocent moonlight stroll with these fellows. No, I'd danced my way right into the middle of the deadly battle about to take place.

The dark man peeled his glare away from Slane and turned his sharp eyes upon me. I decided I must look a sight to him, wearing my twenty-first-century dress compared to his primitive garb. Although, he had easily accepted and analyzed my presence, saying I came from the heavens. Where exactly that may be, in his opinion, I had no idea. I took his assumption as a good thing when he suddenly set down his weapon at his feet.

"She is a gift. Sent as a sign that there be

peace between us," he directed this comment at his foe.

I let loose a breath I'd been holding and looked to see what Slane thought of this announcement. He frowned but soon set down his weapon as well. I stared at the two men who stood rigid, unwilling, or uncertain of what should happen next.

"I am Jekop," the dark man said to me. "Of the Plains."

"I'm Starr."

"He is Slane." He raised his hand, indicating the giant behind me. "Of the Forest."

"We've met."

"So Jekop believes you have come from the heavens." I could hear condescension in Slane's voice.

Jekop narrowed his eyes, and I saw him ball his fists. "You have proven how blind you and the others like you are. You pretend to see nothing or ignore what is right before your face. Starr appeared here like magic. You saw it. I know you did, just as I did. Do not deny it. Not this time."

So, this had been an argument they'd had before. Had others appeared here in this spot just as I had?

"Even her name is heavenly sounding," Jekop continued.

"You are a fool. There is no magic in this place. Starr's presence is strange, but she is a real, live woman. Not a ghost."

Jekop came closer and reached out a wary hand to touch me gently on the arm. When he felt the firmness of my flesh, it seemed to satisfy his curiosity. "Yes, she is real. It is why she is a gift to us. She came when we were set to battle to the death over this land. The gods do not wish for us to quarrel."

"She could have traveled from anywhere. Her presence can be explained," Slane insisted.

"No. She appeared out of nowhere," Jekop said, holding firm to his belief.

It hadn't been nowhere, actually. Yet, I couldn't very well tell them I'd time-traveled. Jekop was eager to believe that I'd appeared to bring peace despite Slane and his suspicions. I was afraid of what might happen if Slane convinced Jekop to doubt me as well.

I decided to swing the odds in my favor. "Jekop is right. The gods have delivered me here to you as a sign of peace between you." I had to do it.

Both of the men took a reverent step

backward. In my sweater, I'd left behind my camera and a cheap cellphone I'd purchased for directions or emergencies while in England. Oh, how I wished for those items. Having them might convince these guys I was from another place. But watching their actions now, I felt they did believe me, especially Jekop, who actually kneeled down and lowered his head.

"What is it the gods wish of us?" Jekop asked me.

Judging by the look on Slane's face, he wasn't convinced my presence was divinely ordained. He drilled me with a look. "Yes, Starr, tell us. What do the gods wish of us?" One of his eyebrows rose, and he crossed his arms over his chest.

"Um, they want you to stop fighting over the land." It had been what Jekop suggested anyway.

"Surely they must propose a solution or a compromise then?" Slane insisted.

"Yeah. Sure. They ah, want you to share it."

Jekop leapt to his feet. "No! That must not be right. This is a holy place where the dead walk. He and his people come here and put up dead trees. It is wrong. Disrespectful."

He waved his hand erratically at Slane and the wooden posts looming around us.

"What is it you're doing here exactly?" I asked Slane.

He ignored me. "I'm disrespectful? What about your people's sacrifices?"

What?

"They are made in honor of the gods," Jekop replied.

"Sacrifices?" I couldn't get past the word.

Suddenly, there was a commotion at the base of the slope behind Jekop. Three men crept forward and stopped to stare at us.

"Jekop, what is happening?" one of the men hissed.

"It is okay. We have been sent a gift from the gods," Jekop said over his shoulder to the men.

"A sacrifice?" another one asked.

"No!" I yelled.

As the men began to creep forward, I felt a hand take mine. When I would have pulled free, it tightened and began to lead me away.

"What are you doing?" I demanded while Slane continued to pull.

"Getting you out of here while Jekop deals with his men."

"But…"

He stopped. "Do you want to be their next sacrifice?"

"Of course not!"

"Then come with me. Now." He began pulling me again, and this time, I went along with him.

We started running when we heard angry voices telling us to stop. We didn't stop until we reached the forest, which, thankfully, unlike in my time, wasn't far from where I'd appeared. Slane slowed down and then stopped when we entered the shelter of the trees.

"It's all right now. They won't follow us in here."

"Why? What's stopping them?" I looked back across the field, and sure enough, Jekop and the three men, along with half a dozen more, stood about twenty yards away as though an invisible barrier prevented them from coming closer.

"They are." Slane lifted his hand to indicate a group of very tall, very blond men who appeared from behind the trees. When I wanted to stand in place and gawk, Slane latched onto me and began tugging again. "We need to go," he said. "Come," he ordered the men, who obediently fell into step behind us.

I tried to get free, but Slane's grip was too strong. "Where are you taking me?"

"To my hut," he replied.

The men behind us were silent, which surprised me, considering their leader had just arrived with a strange girl wearing a silvery dress. Though it must have appeared weird and perhaps even frightening to them, they refrained from asking questions.

Soon, we came upon a slight clearing where five primitive huts were erected in a circular fashion around a fire pit that sat in the middle. A fire crackled away, giving off enough light to see the huts were of a decent size yet appeared hastily built. They were spread out enough to allow for a modicum of privacy. Slane strode up to the doorway of the smallest hut and pushed it open.

"Get inside," he said to me, giving me a push. Before he closed the door, I saw him turn to address the men who were no doubt full of curiosity.

Through the darkness, I could just barely make out what appeared to be the only piece of furniture—a bed set against the left wall. Covered in animal skins and comfortable looking, the sight of it made me suddenly aware of how exhausted I was. Even before traveling through time, I'd had a long, busy day.

A thought occurred to me. Who was to say that I wasn't sleeping right now? Or maybe when I'd been dancing at the stones, I'd slipped and hit my head?

I grew excited with the idea. This being a dream or an unconscious delusion would be far better than believing I'd time-traveled. I mean, what a ridiculous assumption.

Whatever this was, I had to play it out. All I could do was hope and pray that someone woke me soon.

Moments later, Slane came through the doorway holding a lit torch. His face and manner were all businesslike. He shoved the torch into a niche in the wall and turned to stare at me while I stood there awkwardly.

"What exactly were you doing before you came through?" he demanded.

"What?"

"Before you came through the portal, what did you do? How did you turn it on?"

"Pardon?"

He smashed his heavy fist into the palm of his other hand, making a resounding thud around the room. "Tell me!"

"I don't know what you're talking about! What do you mean? What do you want me to say?"

"I want you to tell me how you managed to turn on the portal." He spoke slowly as though I was an idiot.

"All I did was dance at Stonehenge. Something I've dreamt of doing since I was eight years old. I waited until everyone was gone, slipped over the barrier, and danced. The next thing I knew, I was here." *Play along.* I couldn't very well tell him he was a figment of my imagination. *Please let him be a figment of my imagination.*

"The barrier? They have it sealed off? This is bad. They must have figured out what it can do. Others may come."

"The barrier keeps people back. It's for preservation's sake. They allow people through on special tours and for special occasions like the summer and winter solstice. What do you mean they've figured out what it can do? And who are the others you think are coming?"

"Others like yourself, from another place. You must have realized by now you're not where you were a while ago?"

"I know," I said, not caring if it came out like a whine. "All I want is to go home."

Slane's expression registered a flicker of guilt but also something else. He cleared his throat and hardened his expression before he spoke. "It's what I want as well. What all of us here want."

CHAPTER 2
STEP IN TIME

I was confused. "You want me to leave?"

"No, you misunderstand. I mean, *we* want to go home as well."

"If you want to go home, why don't you?" Seemed logical enough.

"We can't return home until the portal is turned back on. That is why I need you to tell me what you did to get here."

"There is no portal. There's only the stones. I mean posts. Well, here it's posts, where I'm from, it's stone."

"And where I'm from, it's steel."

Say what? I could actually feel my mouth drop open. "How is that possible?" This whole thing felt so real. I couldn't help but get swept away in the madness. *Wake up!*

"I'm not from here either. Me and the others you saw outside all came from another time, just as I'm sure you did as well."

Doubt began to creep into my mind. This

couldn't actually be happening. "What year?" I asked once I reminded myself to just go with it. Wherever it may lead me.

"2194. I'm sure a bit farther than you've traveled, considering you said the circle contains stone in your time."

Holy crap!

He frowned with disappointment. "I can see by the look on your face that this surprises you, which leads me to believe this was a random event, not a deliberate act."

"I wouldn't do this on purpose. I had no idea things like this were even possible." Was it possible? Maybe I wasn't dreaming.

"Now you know."

If this was my new reality, things might not be as bad as I'd feared. I wasn't in this alone. I thought for a moment, then an idea occurred to me. "How do you know it's not working now? Since I just came through, I mean." I headed to the door, ready to return to the circle, despite Jekop and his men standing and probably waiting just beyond the trees.

"Once you've arrived, that's it. The way through is closed. The person, or people, traveling must be the ones to turn it on. It can also move side to side, but only in the time you are in. We can already make it do that. What we haven't figured out yet is how to go forward."

I stopped before the door, my hopes dashed. "So then, people can arrive, but they can't leave?" This posed a huge problem for me. It appeared I was trapped just as Slane and his men were.

"That's the problem. Where I'm from, we can maneuver the portal manually since we arranged the steel and the proper controls, but we can only make it go one way. At least we now know where we'll end up. Before that, it was unpredictable. With the right devices in place, we have a semblance of control. It's not perfect, but it's better."

"Let me get this straight. Stonehenge is a time portal, and the posts, then the stones, were put into place as a way of manipulating time jumps?"

"Yes."

This was all too much. It did, however, explain the long-standing question as to why the stones were put there. "So there's no way back?"

"Like I said, it's unpredictable. For now, all we can do is location jump around the time we're in."

"Location jump?"

"From place to place in this time. The side to side movement I spoke about."

"You've been moving around while you're here?" That explained the ghosts Jekop said he'd witnessed.

"There are many portals all over Earth. With certain crystals, we can control which destination we travel to."

"Why are you doing this? Why move around Earth?" As cool as it seemed, it was pointless since we couldn't get home. "Why did you come here at all, considering you knew you couldn't get back?"

"Oh, we'll get back. As soon as you show me what you did to get here. Perhaps we can reverse whatever it was you did to bring ourselves forward in time."

What did I do? How did I manage to open a portal and transport myself back thousands of years in time? There was only one thing I could think of. "I danced."

"Danced?"

"Yes. I did. That's all I did."

Slane contemplated me for a full minute before he spoke. "Show me."

He had to be kidding.

"I'm not going to dance for you." Especially not *that* dance. I'd only ever performed it alone, considering it was extremely provocative and undeniably sexy. The steps and movements emerged from somewhere deep inside of me, the place where the music played. When the music began and I joined with it in dance, it transported me. This time, literally.

Slane didn't take kindly to my refusal. He came up before me, standing so close that I had to tilt my head back to look him in the eye. "You'll do it."

His words sounded so confident that I didn't immediately contradict him. First, I swallowed hard. "No. I won't."

From the corner of my eye, I could detect the slow, deliberate movement of his hand. Before I could react, he grasped the back of my head and a handful of my hair. He pulled my head back, and I winced at the pain. "I have no need of you if you will not show me the dance. Do it, or I will take you to the edge of the forest and hand you to Jekop and that band of savages out there."

The word *sacrifice* sounded in my head again. I closed my eyes. The soft pant of Slane's breath brushed my face. I let myself relax and drift. Deeper. Deeper. To the place where the music played. Softly at first, then more pronounced.

I opened my eyes and looked at Slane. "Release me." I was surprised when he complied. "I'll do it," I said.

He backed away, and I lifted my arms and arched my foot. Blocking everything out but the music, I began to move.

Slane became mere background as I arched and swayed in a gentle rhythm. Conscious of my surroundings and yet unconcerned as I twirled around the room, touching here, brushing there, just as I had the stones. The tempo in my head quickened, and my steps obeyed. The feel of a pelt under my fingertips added to the primal urge my body felt when it moved. I no longer danced for Slane or even myself. I moved for time, my secret lover. A hard surface became my lover's chest, which I caressed to coax. The stiffness of a hide teased the surface of my open palm. A strewn fur under my feet enticed the need to lay with my lover. For a moment, I felt flesh. Real skin, warm and inviting. Sensuously, I trailed my fingers down solid muscle, and I quivered with the thought I had brought time to life, *he* was real. I swayed for only seconds, undecided and somewhat confused, until the music swamped my senses, and I once again moved faster and faster. Until, at last, I came to a complete stop and opened my eyes.

Part of me wished I'd brought myself forward in time, thinking it was perhaps my dance that had transported me, not Stonehenge. I couldn't hide my disappointment when I saw Slane standing before me. Watching me. He had a hunger in his eyes I recognized from men in my time. It frightened me and made me back away from him. I realized it was him I had touched. I could feel a blush heat my cheeks.

He shook his head abruptly as though just awakening from a trance. His face became less animated and more businesslike. "You touched as you moved. Did you lay hands on the stones like that?"

"I believe so. It's the same dance."

"That must be what caused the activation, then. A sequence of touches turned it on and brought you here. I must process this information."

He went over to the bed, knelt down, and reached beneath to pull out a box. He set the box on the pelt covering of the bed and opened it up. He lifted out a device that resembled a wide, flat cellphone with a keypad across the bottom. The buttons made soft beeping noises as he busied his fingers across them. A projection of the stones suddenly appeared in the space overtop the bed. I crept forward, wanting to get a better look.

"It's like a hologram," I said.

"Yes. This device allows us to do many things."

I knelt down beside him, still amazed at what I saw. "Will this help get us home?"

"Perhaps. I'll need you to do the dance again, but this time I'll record it. If I play it backward, you can assimilate the dance and hopefully turn the portal on to go in the other direction." The excitement in his voice made me observe him while he fiddled with the device. He was very handsome when he wasn't scowling.

Pounding on the door made us both jump to our feet. "Enter," Slane said.

The door flew open, revealing one of his men. He seemed very agitated about something.

"Captain, it's the tribe of the plains. They've breached the forest."

"They wouldn't dare!" There was that

scowling face again.

"We are engaged in primitive battle, but there are many of them. Should we…"

"No." Slane lifted his hand and cut him off mid-sentence.

"They demand the return of the goddess." He turned his anxious gaze upon me, and I couldn't help but shiver.

"They cannot have her," Slane said. "Every available man must fight. She must be protected."

"Yes, sir," the man replied and then dashed away.

Slane replaced his device into the box and slid it beneath the bed, then he went to the door and shut it, lowering a plank of wood into slats across it. "Don't worry," he told me.

"Breaching the forest, that's bad, right?" They were desperate to sacrifice me. I could feel it in my bones.

"They've never done it before. Although, they've never had reason to."

Until now.

"Oh no." A terrible thought entered my mind.

Clearly puzzled, Slane regarded me. "You are safe, don't worry."

"I…I'm a virgin." My face felt warm, and I knew I was blushing. It grew even hotter when Slane's expression changed, and he actually raised an eyebrow.

He appeared surprised by my admission. Maybe Jekop wouldn't suspect me of being a virgin, either? If he were to steal me back, it might buy me some time, but how much?

"That could pose a problem," he said, adding to my paranoia. "These people are wild, primitive, and have proven to be unpredictable. Even more so now that you're here."

I didn't like the way he was looking at me. When he took a step forward, I took one back. We continued this game until I could retreat no further. The backs of my knees were in contact with his large, soft bed.

"If the worst happens and Jekop takes you from me, he may sacrifice you. Especially if you're a virgin."

His matter-of-fact words made me tremble in fear. "What can I do?"

"The situation is easily remedied," he whispered as he lifted his hand to the back of my head once more, holding me securely while his lips descended on mine.

I'm sure Slane's kiss would have been

much more enjoyable if there hadn't been a band of ferocious tribesmen battling outside the door, anxious to sacrifice me, so much for me being the bringer of peace. Despite that, I did lose myself for an instant, forgetting all about the world outside that small room. Slane and I became the only two people on Earth. Nothing else mattered. That was until the angry clash of weapons sounded, and the shouts outside became louder. I emerged reluctantly from the hazy, wondrous enjoyment I'd allowed myself to indulge in. Looking into Slane's eyes, I had to remind myself that there were men outside, battling to take me away, determined to sacrifice my life. My virginity, despite being something I'd protected fiercely for years, was now, as crazy as it seemed, putting my life in danger.

"We could run?" I suggested, struggling from his embrace.

"No," Slane said, reaching for me again. "Do not fear. I can breach you quickly. There won't be much discomfort."

How romantic.

I argued feebly while he lowered me to the bed, weakening my reservations with small, soft, ingeniously placed kisses. My silvery dress slipped off easily without much coaxing, along with my lacy bra and panties. Slane's primitive garb came off next. Naked on the bed together, I felt my walls crumble, battered by my partner's eager efforts to save me from myself.

The battle outside became distant, background noise, barely discernible thanks to the sweet melody playing in my head and Slane's sugary words, words my secret lover would say if time could speak. His warm heat made me tingle, and I gasped at the panting breath in my ear. When his hot kisses trailed from my lips and face down to my neck and shoulders, I twined my fingers in his silky hair and concentrated on the slippery, blond wisps. An unexpected moan escaped my mouth as he moved his lips lower and fastened onto my nipple. I froze, humiliated, and shamed that my body responded so willingly to his expert ministration. His heavy thigh thrown over my leg allowed me to feel his erection stir to life. Never had I gone so far in lovemaking before. I'd kissed, of course, and done some heavy petting but never lain naked with a man.

"Do not hide from me," Slane told me, his voice strained and gruff.

Hide? I lay naked beneath him. Where did he think I would go?

"Let go," he said.

I dropped my hands from his hair, figuring I was pulling, and placed my arms at my side.

"No. Touch me," he instructed.

I moved my hands to his hips and held him softly.

"Now, let go." His voice was husky and held an edge.

"Make up your mind." Did he want me to touch him or not?

"Sweet, sweet Starr. Touch me, please, I beg you. When I tell you to let go, I mean give yourself to me. Do not shy from me. If I pleasure you, moan. Cry out when I breach you, for there will be pain."

"Pain?" I stiffened again.

"Only briefly, then pleasure. Oh, such pleasure," he assured me.

My cheeks felt hot. I was embarrassed that he wanted me to moan and cry out. What did he think, that I had absolutely no control over my body? True, I had let one moan slip out, but I refused to do it again despite what he did.

"Holy Mother! What are you doing?" It wasn't a moan! I'd entangled my fingers in his hair again, but while pondering his words, I'd failed to notice how his head had dipped much lower, and now I felt him between my legs. Oh! How I felt him. His lips…they were…there.

"Do you want me to stop?"

"No! I mean, no. If you want to continue, then by all means…ohhh!" There was that hot tongue of his again. It felt so…so wonderful. This wasn't supposed to be a pleasurable interlude between lovers but an act to be quickly done to save my life, yet Slane's gentleness lured my senses into forgetting that fact, if for only a moment or two.

Hearing the battle noises raging outside the door made completing the deed prominent in our minds once more. Slane left the vicinity of my open thighs and ascended back up my body until we were once again face-to-face. Him being so much taller than I, he rose higher until his prick came into contact with my pussy. I braced myself as the tip of his shaft pressed against me.

I reached between us. For brief seconds, I closed my fingers around his thick, long length and realized all of that would soon be buried deep within me. I released him to push at his rock-solid chest. A chest that was pressed against my own, flattening my breasts. I felt his steel thighs and became acutely aware of just how powerful the man on top of me was. The great size of him made me forget my resolve to not moan or make any sounds. "Get off! Get off!" I wiggled wildly while he tried to hold me steady.

"Listen! That is not a card game going on outside. Those are men engaged in mortal combat. Jekop is out there, and he is not going to willingly leave without you. As pleasurable as this is, I would much rather be battling alongside my men who are laying down their lives in primitive combat to keep you safe. Now get ahold of yourself, and let's get this done."

I lay still. The truth of Slane's words rang true. Men were fighting and possibly dying beyond the door to this small lair while I lay relatively safe in the arms of a man willing to spoil me in the name of duty. It wasn't as if he was about to use his power to battle me.

"You're right. Please continue." I wouldn't fight him anymore. Even though that enormous prick of his would surely split me in two, I would lay there and do my duty as well.

He surged forward, filling me so completely until my barrier gave way. I cried out in pain. He stilled and held me until the moment passed. And though the deed was done, he began to move. Ever so gently, he slid himself out before thrusting again. As he moved deeper, I felt my insides stretch to accept him. My breath caught, and I lifted my legs around his waist to keep his formidable thighs from crushing them. His actions confused me. I was safe now. No longer a virgin, and yet he continued. I put my hand on his shoulder, meaning to stop him and tell him to go and call off the battle. Jekop would have no use of me now. I was safe. The fighting could end.

But something changed. The music in my head grew louder as he rocked against me. The sweet melody made me relax, and amazingly, I began to enjoy what Slane was doing. When he started to thrust harder, I caught on and joined his rhythm. My legs tightened around him. My fingers dug into the pelt bedding beneath me. I was right. He wasn't just powerful, he was power itself. His groans and grunts accentuated the primitive hovel. Being from the future, he had taken on the role of primeval man exceptionally well. My body moved for him with the rhythm that built within me. My fingers touched him, my palms stroked against his sweat-moistened skin. Was Slane my secret lover? I danced beneath him in my first duet.

He, not being insensitive to the precariousness of the situation outside, determinedly stroked, quickly bringing me to completion. I did yell then. Loudly. Moments later, Slane's breath became quicker, and he actually growled as he pulled out of me and spent his passion on my stomach. When he finally stilled we stared each other in the eye.

"It's done," he said, with the nerve to wink at me.

I blinked, feeling heady and drunk and a wee bit confused until I came to my senses.

"Get off and go out there!" I snapped, suddenly embarrassed to be lying naked beneath him, covered in his desire. "You can stop all this right now. Tell Jekop I'm no longer a virgin, and I cannot be sacrificed."

Slane rose from the bed and donned his clothing in a hurry. He passed me a slip of cloth to clean off my belly and bloodied thighs and then went to unbar the door. He paused to study me while I slipped on my undergarments and pulled my dress over my head. "Do you really think Jekop will leave without you?"

"Of course. I'm no good to him now."

"He thinks you are a goddess, sent from

the heavens to bring peace between our people."

"He also wants to sacrifice me."

"We don't know that for sure."

I pushed the hair from my face and began to hastily fashion one long braid over my shoulder. "What the hell do you mean? We just did it because you said my virginity could be a problem."

"That's right. I said it *could* be a problem."

I stared at him in shock. "You asshole! You don't think he wants to sacrifice me at all, do you?"

He shrugged his shoulders. "Maybe he will, maybe he won't. I never know what Jekop is thinking or what he will do next."

"But you don't think he's the type to sacrifice a woman he believes is a goddess sent to bring peace?"

"That would be counterproductive, don't you think?" Before I could respond or even throw something at his arrogant head, he lifted the bar from the door and placed it aside. "Replace this after me." He slipped through the door and shut it tight.

Did he expect me to just hang around? Wait for the fighting to end and wordlessly become the spoils to the victor? I was mad.

Royally pissed, actually. But what was I to do?

I went to the door and replaced the bar. As much as it galled me, there was nothing else I could do except wait. Feeling completely exhausted again, I lay down on Slane's bed and rested my head on his pillow. The noise outside made it impossible to relax. I pulled the fur up over my head in an attempt to muffle the sound, but it was futile.

The next thing I knew, the door was being pummeled. If Slane was at the door, he wouldn't be throwing himself against it. No, he would knock and ask me to let him in. So, it must be the enemy.

A moment later, I realized my reasoning was correct as the door shattered to pieces, and Jekop forced himself into the room. His gaze swept around and came to fasten on me, sitting up terrified in Slane's bed. He strode over and knelt before it. "I will protect you with my life, Goddess. This is my solemn vow. Please come, Starr." He reached out his hand to me. The fierce expression on his face might have made me fight him, but it was the determination I saw in his eyes that swayed me.

Ass that Slane was, he would come for me. Though he had manipulated my fears, I had touched him when I danced with more than just my hands. I had drawn him into my secret world, and like Savannah, I had gripped his heart until it beat for me. I knew with all certainty it would beat for me again.

What else could I do but put my hand in Jekop's and trust that I made the right decision? He led me from the room with utmost care and haste. We escaped like thieves into the forest while his and Slane's men continued to fight.

CHAPTER 3
STEP IN TIME

Over my shoulder, I caught a brief glimpse of the raging battle going on around the huts and campfires as Jekop pulled me along behind him. We escaped into the thickness of the trees and continued on until I could no longer keep up with his pace. He slowed when I tugged at his hand, lagging behind, my legs about ready to give out. There was a small, running stream steps away, and he led me over beside it and knelt down.

"Drink." Cupping his hands, he demonstrated the technique as if I'd never attempted something so primitive before.

I went down beside him and waited to catch my breath.

"He should not have taken you." I could feel his eyes on me while I drank.

We were in agreement there. Or were we? What if my fear about Jekop became a reality? Staring into his earnest face, I had to make myself believe he wouldn't be capable of hurting me. The only way to find out was to face this head-on.

"He was concerned for my safety. Especially when he heard your man talk of sacrifice."

I watched Jekop's expression with trepidation for any revealing hints of his intentions. When his face registered shock, my shoulders sagged in relief. His gaze softened, and I knew he had seen my fear.

"You are the goddess, sent to bring peace between the people of the forest and my people of the plains," he reminded me. "That you would follow me willingly even though you thought I might cause you harm speaks of great fealty to the gods. You do them proud."

"Thanks." It was probably in my best interests to allow Jekop to go on believing I was heaven sent. Suspicions of me had already been tossed out there and shot down, so I didn't think he would accept the truth. It was all so very exhausting, this lying and fleeing for my life. Not to mention losing my virginity. All I wanted to do was sleep and go home. At the moment I didn't care in which order.

"Forgive me, you are weary. There is

shelter nearby where we can rest in safety." He got to his feet and offered me his hand.

Once I stood before him, I let loose a great sigh. "Okay, lead the way."

He smiled down at me. "It is not far." He escorted me off once again in the opposite direction of Slane's camp.

Not much later, we ascended a slight stony hilltop dotted with trees. Jekop stopped before a rock face and fiddled around with some brush, revealing a concealed opening in the rock. The entrance was narrow and low, and we had to duck our heads to gain entry to the dark interior. Jekop recovered the entryway as best he could. The full moon had guided our steps through the night outside, but now it was blocked from view, leaving us in complete darkness.

"I can't see," I complained as Jekop began guiding me onward. He stopped all of a sudden, and I plowed into his back. I felt him turn, his arms moving gently around me to offer comfort.

"It is all right. The cave is deep. Just a few more steps, and I can make light to warm us and allow us to see."

I assumed he meant he'd light a fire.

"Can't you do it now?" The cave was damp, chilling my skin which was still slightly sweaty from our flight.

"We must go farther, or the light may be detected from outside."

I wanted to stomp my foot in frustration, not caring if it was childish. "Let's hurry. I'm cold."

We walked on, Jekop keeping one of his thick arms around me. Finally, several steps later, we stopped. He guided me to sit down, and I could hear him rustling around in the dark. A series of smacks sounded, and I assumed he was trying to create a spark with some flint. Soon a tiny flame leapt to life, which he nurtured in his cupped hands with bits of moss and what appeared to be animal hair. As the flame grew stronger, he lowered it to a small circle of stones I could now decipher. I reached out my hands, welcoming the warmth, while he stoked the blaze with small pieces of dry wood stacked neatly nearby.

As the area grew more visible, I checked out my surroundings. I was seated on one of three flat stones placed near the fire pit. Behind me, almost obscured by shadows, was a spot piled with furs. I assumed this was the sleeping area. I also noticed it seemed to be the only one.

"I need to rest," I told him.

"Go, lie down and put many furs on you. It will grow cold. I cannot keep the fire high, or the smoke will become too thick."

Not needing to be told twice, I scrambled to the furs and buried myself in them as Jekop had instructed. Before I remembered courtesy and thought to offer him a fur, I fell fast asleep and didn't awaken until morning. At least, I figured it was morning since the cave seemed brighter. I got up and went to the fire. Jekop appeared to be asleep on the ground, but I had a feeling if I were to move any further, he would suddenly spring wide-awake. I cleared my throat a couple of times to get his attention. When he sat up and smiled at me, I smiled back.

"I need to ah…" I knew my face was flaming, but matters couldn't be helped. I wondered if my need to pee would be considered un-goddess-like and give me away.

Jekop didn't seem to find my request unusual. He gestured to the back right of the cave. "Follow the path, and it will take you deeper into the cave. There, you will find many areas for privacy."

I wandered off and soon found a suitable

location. When I returned to the fire pit, Jekop was standing and appeared to be ready to leave.

"It should be safe to return to camp now," he told me. Instead of heading back in the direction we had come from last night, he led me deeper into the cave, the same way I'd just returned from moments before.

"Why are we going this way?" I asked.

"There are many exits from this cave, coming out in different places."

Curious, but not unusual. I'd been through a few caves in my childhood when one of my friends, whose family had a cottage up north, had taken me away for the odd weekend. We'd explored some old mining caves, but nothing compared to this.

"Why do your people live on the plains, exposed to threats of the elements and other tribes, when you could live here?" There was more than enough room.

"For many years, my ancestors lived here, as did we. Now, we have chosen to live more closely to the stones. It is the will of the gods who have shown us their presence."

Poor, misguided people. If they only knew the strange comings and goings they'd witnessed were Slane and his men — their mortal enemies — I was sure they would feel differently. I didn't wish to enlighten him, though, not considering my only hope of returning home was to get back to Slane.

Thinking of Slane, I grew annoyed and all tingly at the same time. That I had suspected he'd manipulated me into sleeping with him in the guise of keeping me safe rang much truer with a clear morning head. Giving him the benefit of the doubt for a moment, I supposed it could be possible he had truly been afraid for me, as he'd said, considering he'd left his men battling outside to be with me. I knew it'd been difficult for him. He'd not been able to conceal his worry. So perhaps there was some truth to his actions?

When we entered Jekop's camp, everyone seemed to light up with excitement. Judging from the young children who ran up to greet him and the smiles and extended hands from the men and women, I could see Jekop was well-loved and admired. In contrast, I wouldn't exactly describe Slane's men as being loving toward him. I'd more describe them as deferential and perhaps fearful. It was the feeling I'd gotten. Slane was so different from Jekop. Where Slane was cool and calculating,

Jekop was all heat and passion. They were like fire and ice.

We came to a stop before the fire pit. Tent-like structures nestled together around it, I assume for practical and defensive reasons, much like Slane's camp. The dwellings were cone-shaped and covered by animal skins and bark, much sturdier in appearance than Slane's huts were. They also had twice as many, taking the women and children they needed to accommodate into account.

Some men came forward and encircled us, and the women and children moved off into the background. I looked around at the faces of the men and wondered which one had asked about me being sacrificed. If the suggestion were raised again, I'd probably blurt out that I was no longer a virgin. Damn my reputation.

"Jekop, you have returned the goddess to us!" a wizened old man said. The men cheered over these words.

"Yes, now we shall have peace at last," Jekop said. His words were hopeful, but his face looked anything but. I guess he was remembering all the fighting he and the others had done last night.

"What about the men of the forest? Will

they not seek the return of the goddess?" This question made Jekop look even more doubtful.

The men began speaking all at once, making excited comments and firing questions at Jekop, who did his best to answer. All the while, I stood there feeling very conspicuous in my shiny dress. The men didn't look worse for wear, considering the battle that had gone on last night. I was relieved. I didn't want anyone getting hurt on account of me. Especially when they had come to rescue me under false pretenses.

Things settled down moments later when one of the women called out that the morning meal was ready. My stomach growled loudly at the announcement, reminding me I hadn't eaten since my arrival.

Jekop led me to his tent and settled me down inside on his nest of furs. "I will bring you food and water," he said, then slipped away.

After a breakfast consisting of coarse bread, fresh eggs, and strips of dried meat I found immensely satisfying, he brought me a tunic similar to the ones the women at camp wore.

"It is not fit for a goddess," he stated, seeing the curious look on my face.

"No, it's perfect." After wearing my dress all day and night, I was more than happy to have something else to put on.

He left me alone to change, and when he returned, he smiled shyly as I tugged on the short hem of the outfit. Together, we went out, and he led me around and introduced me to his people. My change of clothing made my appearance less daunting, and I found I was quickly and warmly welcomed. The pace of the camp was slow and easy, and the day passed without any disturbances.

That night, not long after the evening meal, taken companionably around the campfire, Jekop led me back to his tent.

"Where will you sleep?" I asked him. He had barely left my side all day.

"Do not fear, Starr. I will be here, just outside the door. You are safe."

I did feel safe with him nearby. But as I nestled down deep into the soft furs and felt sleep begin to overtake me, I grew worried. How long would Slane be content to wait? I had what he wanted — needed — to get home. And I knew he wouldn't be patient.

* * * *

It took a week for Slane to make his move.

While a group of us sat together by the fire, telling stories in soft voices, mindful of the children that mothers had just tucked in for the night, a line of lit torches abruptly appeared at the edge of the forest. In the center of the line stood the tallest, broadest, and most ferocious of the men. Slane. Across the plain, through the gradually dimming light, I could almost feel his cold eyes boring right into me, even from the distance. He stood firm and unyielding. I wasn't sure if I should be glad or terrified.

The past week spent getting to know Jekop and his people had been an incredible experience. I was suddenly reluctant to leave this simple, happy life despite living in the rough, which, as a city girl, was something I was definitely not used to. I'd found real enjoyment in my days. And my nights. Spending time getting to know this gentle yet fiercely protective tribe had been an unexpected joy. They'd welcomed me into their midst. A stranger. And though they thought of me as a goddess, that hadn't stopped them from handing me a bowl of vegetables to scrub or a pot to rinse clean.

After so many years of searching, I'd finally found a place I felt I belonged. My world had offered me the theater and the stage. And the dance. But it had been a solitary life. Each night, I'd come home by myself. Even when surrounded by others, I'd somehow still been alone. I didn't feel like that here. Seeing Slane appear across the field reminded me of my old life and made me ask myself just how anxious I was to reclaim it.

The fourth night I was at camp, Jekop had taken up my invitation to come sit with me on the furs in his tent. Just to talk. He'd been shy with me at first, well aware of our scantily clad bodies and our close confines. When he'd ducked his head in shyness, I'd brushed a fallen lock of black hair from his face.

"Tell me about you, Starr," he said to me, adoration gleaming in his eyes.

"What do you want to know?" It was hard not to like a man who thought everything you said and did was divine. Yet I had to be careful answering his questions. My precarious situation made my belly knot up in dread whenever I thought too much about it. I'd given up my fanciful thoughts of this being a dream or a delusion. I'd had to admit this was all very real.

He leaned back, resting his arms behind him. "Tell me about the heavens. Are they as beautiful as we imagine?"

"I don't know."

His expression became puzzled. "How can that be? Do you mean you do not remember?"

I shrugged. Deceiving him was so difficult. I didn't want to do it anymore.

He appeared to give this matter great thought for a moment or two. "We saw you appear. Even though Slane denies this fact, I know it to be true. I believe he does as well, or else he would not have run off with you. Did he question you?"

I wasn't sure how much I should reveal. "Um, yes. He wanted to know how I appeared at the stones."

"And what did you tell him?"

"I was dancing."

"Dancing?"

Jekop already believed I came from the heavens. How much harder would it be to convince him that I came from someplace else? I knew he'd be disappointed, but it would put an end to the lies.

"I don't exactly know how I got here. Although I'm sure it was the dance that brought me. I come from another place. Another world.

Not from the heavens."

"Another world?"

"Actually, another time. I'm from the future. I'm sorry."

Though a million questions must have been burning in his mind for an answer, he remained silent. At least he hadn't run off in fear. However, judging by the great size of him, I couldn't imagine him ever being afraid of anything.

"Please say something." His silence made me uneasy.

"You arrived the moment Slane and I were to fight to the death. Though you say you come from the future, I still believe you were sent here to bring peace."

"You think the gods brought me here?" And I thought it was just my crazy dancing.

"Yes. But I no longer believe you to be a goddess."

Was that a good thing or a bad thing? He wasn't going to sacrifice me now, was he?

"No, I'm just a woman."

"And I am a man." Jekop's voice was suddenly husky, and he had a predatory gleam in his eye.

Instead of fearing him I felt a heat fuse

through my body, something I now recognized as anticipation. He lifted his hand and reached out to touch my hair. His touch was like fire, and my skin burned as he trailed his fingers over my cheek, across my throat, and then down my arm.

"I want you, Starr," he said.

"I want you too."

He reached for me and laid me back gently on the soft fur, keeping me nestled in the warmth of his arms. He lowered his head, and his lips brushed mine. I kissed him back, reaching up to entangle my fingers in his hair.

His kiss was achingly sweet. I savored it, snuggling in his arms. Slane's lovemaking had been hurried due to the circumstances we'd faced. But there was no battle raging outside now. I wanted to linger in Jekop's embrace. To touch, explore, know every inch of him as I had been denied knowing Slane. I became brave and turned Jekop so that it was he who lay back on the furs. Boldly, I removed every stitch of his clothing until he was exposed before me in all his beautiful glory. I ran my hands and lips over his body. His belly was rock-hard muscle, yet his skin felt like silk. Lower I explored, handling his impressive prick with both my hands. He was rock-hard there, too.

"I...I cannot..." Sitting up suddenly, he lifted me, flipping me over onto my back. My tunic went flying off next, and then I was the one lying exposed and vulnerable. When I thought he would take me, plunging deep inside, he surprised me by throwing my legs up over his broad shoulders and lowering his head to my core.

"Oh!" It was my turn to squirm. Two of his thick fingers pushed inside of me while his lips wreaked havoc with my clit. "Jekop, please," I begged.

Taking mercy on me, he rose. Keeping my legs over his shoulders, he gripped my hips and then raised them up to meet his thrust. He plunged deeply, filling me so completely I gasped with the intensity I felt. Sweet music filled my head while his hips kept time with the tempo. Faster and faster the music played, and faster Jekop moved. When I came, I swear I saw stars overhead, as though we had been transported outside beneath the night sky. Jekop hollered his release moments later, and we rode out our bliss as one.

"I love you, Starr," he said, collapsing beside me.

"I love you, too." In the moment, I truly felt as though I did love him. Lying in his arms, I felt content and happy for the first time in my life.

The fearful, anxious voices around the fire made me suddenly snap back into the present. Slane stood out there with armed men ready to fight to reclaim me. My gaze flashed to Jekop, who now stood tall and strong before me, ready to meet Slane in battle. If I didn't do something, lives might be lost. Because of me.

I had to think. Had to act.

As Jekop began issuing commands to his men, I reached out and caught him by the hand. "Please don't go," I begged him.

"I must."

"No! There must be another way." There had to be.

Instead of brushing off my words, as I feared he might, he gave me his full attention. "I do not wish to fight, but I will to protect you. To protect peace."

If he only knew how ironic that sounded. Throughout the ages, men seemed forever to wage battles in the name of peace.

"You and I can walk out there and meet Slane with no weapons. I was with him long enough to know he's a man of honor. If he sees just us two, he will come forward. We can talk. We can have peace by talking, just the three of us." When he appeared reluctant over the idea I continued. "Please, Jekop. It's the only way."

A moment later, he dropped his head and sighed. I knew I had won.

"Stop," he told the men who were arming up, preparing for battle. "Starr and I will meet their champion alone. We will talk peace." He looked at me and smiled.

While the men grumbled and fidgeted, uncertain what they should do, I clasped Jekop's hand in mine and led him toward the field and the awaiting line of torches at the edge of the forest.

I could only hope that Slane was what I'd claimed him to be — a man of honor.

CHAPTER 4
STEP IN TIME

The people of the forest watched us come across the field. When they saw we were alone, Slane ventured away from his men and headed toward us. We met in the center of the field. It was dark now, although the clear sky and bright moon, along with the glow of Slane's torch, allowed us to see each other clearly enough.

"You are wise to return Starr to me," Slane said to Jekop.

I felt Jekop's grip on my hand tighten as he bristled over Slane's arrogant tone. "We have come to talk of peace," Jekop said.

Slane's laughter was cold and cruel. "Peace? What peace? Just give her to me and go."

"You will not take her from me," Jekop told him.

Nothing was going to be solved this way. Not with these two bullheaded warriors acting like this. I let go of Jekop's hand and stood between the two giants, who had puffed out their chests in anger.

"Hold on! Both of you. I am not anyone's property, and I don't have to go with either of you."

"You need me as much as I need you," Slane informed me.

"Don't flatter yourself," I snapped. "We came out here to talk peace, and that's what we're gonna do." I turned to Jekop. "Let's go to the caves, where we can sit down and talk in private."

Jekop nodded in agreement and began to stride away. I followed along behind him, jogging to keep up with his quick pace.

When I looked over my shoulder and noticed Slane remained standing, now with his arms crossed, I sent him a pleading look. "Come on!"

"Oh, very well," he snapped. "Go to camp and await my return," he hollered to his men and then began to follow Jekop and me.

A while later we reached one of the openings to the cave. Jekop ventured inside. Not fearing us being followed, he lit a torch he found just inside the entrance to guide our way. Once Slane and I joined him, Slane finally spoke for the first time since we'd headed out.

"This is incredible," he exclaimed, looking around in awe.

"I know, it is," I agreed.

Jekop frowned at both of us. "I will make more light up ahead, and we can make peace between us."

Slane looked ready to argue, but when I put my hand lightly on his arm, he settled. We continued to follow Jekop. He led us to the fire pit we had camped around when he first brought me to the cave. Using his lit torch, it took him but a few minutes to get a blaze started. Slane stuck his torch into the dirt beside Jekop's, and both of us sat down on the flat rocks. When Jekop was satisfied with the fire, he sat back on his heels and regarded us.

"I believe the way to peace between us begins with sharing," Jekop began.

"That sounds like a good idea," I agreed when Slane remained silent. The grumpy look on his face made me wonder if this had been a good idea after all. "Don't you think it sounds like a good idea, Slane?"

"Huh? Yes, I guess so." I think he was more interested in getting home to the future than he was about peace.

"Starr and I have lain together," Jekop announced.

I gaped, open-mouthed, at him while Slane burst out with a laugh.

"That is hardly appropriate," I snapped, my face flaming.

Ignoring the both of us, Jekop continued. "I believe the way to peace is for us to join together. As one."

"What does that mean?" I asked. I turned to Slane and gave him a swat because he was suddenly grinning from ear to ear.

"It means he wants us to share. Each other," Slane said.

"I believe it to be the only way." Jekop's eyes pleaded with me.

The audacity of these two astounded me. "You expect me to lay with both of you? At the same time?"

"Yes," Jekop and Slane said together. They actually looked at each other and smiled.

"By sharing you, we will join our people. Joined villages are family, and we will not war with family," Jekop said, now serious.

"But you think they are desecrating your land," I sputtered.

"Perhaps the land was speaking to

them," Jekop began thoughtfully. "You are here. I believe through efforts on both sides you came to us. That means you are meant for both."

"Maybe Jekop is right." When Slane said that, I thought he'd wink at me again, but he didn't. He sat looking just as thoughtful as Jekop. Good God, they'd have me believing it soon.

"Dancing pleases the gods, Starr, and you are very pleasing." Jekop's warm gaze washed over me when he said that.

Sex with two men? I had wanted both men before, separately. Why not both now, together? I could feel my heart pound a steady rhythm beneath my ribcage. My teeth clicked together from excitement as it built like the moments before a performance.

Jekop came forward and led me to the nest of furs. Slane was right behind us. I concentrated on the soft fur beneath my feet, willing myself to stay calm. The hair at the nape of my neck was brushed aside, and I felt Slane's warm kisses against my heated flesh. My body shuddered, and goosebumps dotted my arms. Jekop's mouth covered mine. He tasted like the sweet fermented beverage his people liked to indulge in on occasion. Slane moved his fingers against the tie of my tunic to expose my shoulder, and as the tunic slipped lower, my breasts were also exposed. The way his mouth attacked my skin, nipping and laving, I thought for certain he tasted me with intent to devour. Jekop filled his hands with my breasts. He pulled my nipples into tight buds and teased them mercilessly.

Both men stripped off their clothing. I raised my hands and floundered helplessly for a moment, wondering who would touch first and where. Jekop made my decision as he captured my fingers and brought them to his stiff erection. My tunic soon pooled at my feet. This was really going to happen.

Jekop took my shoulders and gently pushed me to my knees. His hard prick was right before my face. He stood and waited, allowing me to make my own decision. I reached up and wrapped my fingers around his shaft and, in my innocence, squeezed too tight. He groaned and placed his hand over mine. Back and forth, he moved my hand until I did it on my own. He was so smooth and hard. Becoming bolder, I took him into my mouth. As my lips closed over him, I quivered when strong hands slid down my back to my hips and lower. Slane's finger began caressing my clit, and a moan escaped from deep in my throat. My thighs felt wet with heat, and my need grew.

"Oh," I cried out when Slane's finger, moist with a slick substance, slid carefully into my behind.

"It's all right, Starr. The grease will make this easier," Slane said.

The words registered slowly. Grease? Slane must carry a lined pouch like Jekop did. The grease was used to put in soapstone bowls with tight moss wicks when added light was needed. They used it for cooking and various other necessities. And now, apparently, this.

The feel of Slane's probing finger was a different sensation, and I wiggled against him, uncertain whether I wanted him to stop or continue. Jekop bent me forward onto my hands and knees. I gripped the fur beneath my fingers tight when Slane began to enter me in the rear. He moved slowly, gently easing forward, allowing me to get used to him. In the firelight, I saw my knuckles whiten when I clenched my fists.

"Relax, Starr," Slane said.

Is he kidding?

Soft, soothing words and caresses from

Jekop encouraged me to breathe deeply and calm myself. Soon, Slane was deep inside of me, and he began to move. He put his arm around my waist and pulled me up against his broad chest, positioning me so they could both satisfy themselves. Jekop spread my legs wide and moved between them so that his chest pressed against mine. Slowly, he pushed his prick up inside me.

Oh God. It was like nothing I had ever experienced before. Both men held me tightly, claiming me together. I clasped one hand around Jekop's neck and the other back behind me so I could pull Slane closer. They moved as one.

For Jekop this was so much more, I realized. He honestly thought they were forging two families through me. This wasn't fair to him.

"Slane?" My word was whispered, and saddened.

"It will be fine," he replied in a gentle tone.

I wasn't certain if he was trying to calm me in this new experience or if he heard the confused sense of impending loss in my tone. How could I lose Jekop now?

"You will be fine, Starr." It was now Jekop's turn to soothe me.

Jekop pulled himself free of me and lay back. Slane also withdrew, and with his help, I was soon straddled over Jekop. My body tensed as Jekop once more plunged deep inside me. I cried out. Slane bent me over Jekop and rubbed at my back and behind, then entered me slowly. Jekop's arms wrapped around me to hold me tight as Slane's pace increased. I was being kept safe, warm, and loved. I abandoned my fears.

Overwhelming waves of intense emotions washed over me as I struggled to breathe. Jekop bucked beneath me and I strove to match his pace as Slane set his own. The strength of the hands holding me was a comfort. My breasts were crushed to Jekop's chest as Slane pushed my hips down, and I could feel Jekop grinding against me. Sweat rolled in rivulets from my shoulder blades, and I could see a fine line of wetness formed across Jekop's luxurious hair at his temples.

When Slane roared a release from behind me, I shuddered, and my tension mounted. A scream built in my throat, and I came hard at the same time Jekop did. Spent, I lay across Jekop like a wet dishtowel. I couldn't move, but my mind was flowing with thoughts. I wasn't sorry by any means.

Jekop carefully rolled me to my side. With my face buried in the crook of his shoulder and Slane cuddled to my back, I drifted to sleep with the exquisite feel of soft fur warming me. I was safe in the arms of two powerful protectors.

* * * *

"I will bring food," Jekop said the next morning. He kissed me long and hard and then smiled at Slane before he sauntered off.

I had to admit that after last night, I was feeling remarkably peaceful. Exhausted as well but in a good way.

Slane snatched my hand as soon as Jekop was out of sight. "We need to leave."

"What? Why would you want to leave?" We had bonded last night, the three of us. I was sure of it.

"There is much I didn't get to tell you before Jekop stole you away. My world—people are dying. We came here not only to establish the time route but to return with medicine that no longer exists in my world or even yours."

"Medicine? For what? What's wrong, Slane?" The desperate look on his face made me fearful. This wasn't a ploy.

"Time is of the essence. Every moment wasted means more deaths. Please, come with me."

How could I refuse? As Slane began leading me away, I glanced over my shoulder, with one last look of regret, at the pile of furs. Our love nest. When Jekop returned he would find us gone. I could only hope and pray that, in time, he would forgive us.

Slane led me back in the direction of his camp. "We will get the device and record your dance the way we planned," he told me. "While you've been distracting Jekop, I've been busy making preparations to leave."

I stumbled and almost fell while trying to keep up. The way he spoke about me distracting Jekop made it seem like we were co-conspirators in his plan. I didn't like it.

"You need to tell me what's going on." There was a stream ahead. I knelt down to drink, not worrying about Slane leaving me behind. Sure enough, he turned back and joined me at the water's edge.

After I splashed my face a few times and ran my wet hands through my tangled hair, I sat back on my heels and stared at him. Most of his chest was visible since he wore a short tunic with only one side coming up over his shoulder. At least he got to wear it over animal hide pants. Jekop hadn't given me any of those.

"The medicine you spoke of, what is it?" I asked.

"The plant silphium."

"Silphium?"

"It comes from Cyrenaica. In your time the land is named Libya. It was, or I guess I should say, will be, highly coveted by ancient Greeks. Even their coins will bear a picture of the plant. It's said to cure many diseases, but will be mostly used for quartan fever — malaria."

"Malaria?"

"Running rampant in my world." He kept his sharp gaze on the land around us, ever anxious of discovery. "Let's go."

"Wait. Why not use quinine? Don't you have any?"

"We did, but our supplies are depleted. Cinchona trees are extinct in my time and the synthetic quinine proved ineffective." When I opened my mouth to question him further, he continued. "We could spend a lot of time locating the trees and peeling the bark off of them, but our studies show the silphium plant is just as useful. We can cultivate the plants quickly and successfully, which seems the most viable solution to the problem." He began to walk, and I followed.

"How do you plan to gather the plant if it's so far away? Did you find some here?" I asked while trotting along beside him.

"Remember I told you we can use crystals to location jump in this time?"

"Oh yeah."

"The plants have already been gathered. We transported the logs into the circle the same way. All is ready now. We just need to turn the portal on."

"That's where I come in," I said, hoping it was true.

When we reached his camp, Slane spent only a few minutes talking with his men. Then he slipped into his hut and came out with a sack slung over his shoulder, which must have held the device.

"We'll meet after dark at the portal," were Slane's final words to his men. He gestured to me to follow him and then we were off again. "You and I will record the dance somewhere else. It's not safe here. It's the first place Jekop will look for us."

We walked for quite a while before Slane

was comfortable we were in a safe location. He pulled the sack off his shoulder and set it by his feet. He knelt down and began rifling through it, then passed me a hunk of something wrapped in coarse paper. I unwrapped it and saw it was a piece of food resembling bread.

"It's crude but hearty," he said, pulling out a piece for himself.

I sat down across from him and began to eat. It was actually pretty good.

"So, what's the plan?" I asked.

"Dance, I'll record it, and we learn to do it backward."

"Then we can go home?"

"If it turns the portal on, we can jump forward."

The way he said *jump forward* concerned me. "How far will we jump?"

"With only the logs in place, we should move about a thousand years or so."

"A thousand years?" Not quite far enough.

"Or more."

"But I need to go about *five* thousand years or more. So do you." I let lose a big sigh. Would I never get back? Then again, why would I even want to leave at all? Why risk leaving a place that I was getting to know and like for an unknown world in the future? Why leave a man I was beginning to love? I had deep feelings for Slane now as well, but leaving Jekop was going to rip my heart out.

"Once we jump ahead, we can start the next phase of the cog."

"The cog?"

"Placing the blue stones at the portal." Finished with his bread, Slane stood up. I finished mine as well, sensing he was anxious to begin our dancing lesson.

I'd read about how Stonehenge was constructed in different phases spanning thousands of years. After the logs, there'd been blue stones set in place, and then the mammoth stones that still remained, for the most part, in my time. The word cog seemed to fit. A computer-generated view of Stonehenge from above, when complete, did somewhat resemble the mechanism of a clock.

"But why not build the entire thing now?" I asked. "Then we could go right home."

"It was difficult enough getting the logs into place. Jekop and his people are far too suspicious. Plus, if we were to put everything together now, we would only move from my time to here."

"Defeating the purpose of a time route, I suppose?"

"Yes. My world is becoming difficult and even dangerous to live in. Most resources have been depleted. War and disease are out of control. If we distribute groups throughout time, our presence will be less noticeable or intrusive."

"I see." He'd given me a lot to think about. But for now, we had a vital next step to complete. I started to limber up so I'd be ready to dance. "I'll be ready in a few."

Slane bent down to retrieve his device from the sack. He pulled it out and began fiddling with it. "Okay, I'm ready when you are."

"Is here all right?"

"Yes."

I lifted my arms up over my head and arched my foot. When I closed my eyes, I stilled completely, blocking out all sounds around me, concentrating only on my breath. The music began shortly after. Softly at first, then becoming more prominent. Like a good and trusted friend, I knew it would be there, never letting me down. Forgetting Slane's eyes were on me, I began the movements that had brought me here to this time.

Minutes later, as the dance came to completion, I gradually became aware of my surroundings once more. I lowered my hands and opened my eyes. Slane's gaze was fastened upon me as I knew it would be. I dropped my gaze, breaking eye contact. The hunger I'd witnessed in his face made me want to grab his hand and rush back to find Jekop, to engage once again in the lovemaking we had last night.

"Did you get it?" I asked, gesturing to his device.

Slane pushed a few buttons, and a holographic image appeared before him. I came around to witness what he was seeing. The image of myself dancing was haunting. I'd never seen this dance before, and I must admit, it stunned me. It appeared magical and breathtaking. No wonder it had the power to move me through time. When it was over, Slane cleared his throat loudly, breaking the spell.

"Now in reverse," he said. Pushing a few more buttons, the image of me began to move once more, this time in reverse. I thought it would look funny the way a movie does when you see people moving backward, but if anything, the dance looked even more beautiful. We watched it a few more times until I felt I knew how to assimilate the steps.

"Ready?" I asked him.

Slane nodded once and then shut off his device and returned it to the sack.

"Watch me first, then do as I do," I said.

I closed my eyes and waited for the music in my head. Once it started, I began to move. In my mind's eye, I replayed the image of the dance and followed along. When the dance was over, I opened my eyes. I knew I would have to keep watch on Slane while he learned the steps, though it would feel strange doing the dance with my eyes open.

Slane came up before me. "What should I do?" he asked.

For someone who'd probably never danced before, he seemed eager, not nervous. I, however, was uncertain. Dancing with Slane would be like an invitation to him into my world. A place no one had ever truly been before. I'd danced on stage with others, but we had performed steps in a show. This dancing I did on my own was different, being mine alone. Slane and I had made love, but somehow, I knew dancing with him would be even more intimate.

He went behind me, and when I lifted my arms up over my head, I sensed him mirroring my actions. We moved slowly so Slane could follow along. Whenever I caught a glimpse of him swaying or stepping, his gracefulness surprised me. He was a natural, it seemed. It didn't take more than half a dozen run-throughs before he had the dance mastered.

"You're good," I told him. If he lived in my time, I think he would have made an excellent dance partner. "I guess I shouldn't be surprised, considering your other talents." I winked at him.

He nodded at my praise, taking it as his due. If anything, he preened a little. "We'll wait for nightfall and then meet with the others at the portal."

"So, we're going to leave then? Just like that?"

He shrugged. "Yes."

What about Jekop, I wanted to demand, but the businesslike look on Slane's face made my words freeze up. He bent to pick up his sack and then took it over with him to sit down, his back leaning against a tree. He retrieved his device from the sack and turned all his attention to it.

"Get some rest," he said to me without even looking up.

Having nothing else to occupy me, I did as Slane suggested and settled down nearby, leaning against a tree as well. I closed my eyes and tried to rest, refusing to think about jumping a thousand years or more into the future and leaving Jekop behind.

CHAPTER 5
STEP IN TIME

Come nightfall, we all met as agreed at Stonehenge. Slane's men stood ready, loaded down by what I assumed were sacks of silphium. They were armed and appeared eager for the next stage of their journey.

With the turmoil going on inside me it seemed somewhat anticlimactic that the surrounding land was so peaceful. Where was Jekop? Had he even bothered to search for Slane and me? He didn't know our plans, of course. Yet I'd hoped that somehow he'd figured out what we were up to. I longed to see him standing large and defiant at the posts, just daring us to leave him. But it wasn't to be.

"I make no guarantees this will work," Slane addressed the men. "Stand prepared either way."

He was really going to do it. Leave. Without saying goodbye.

Slane walked up to the center of the posts

and gestured for me to join him. I backed away.

"What are you doing?" he demanded. "We must leave. Now. Before Jekop and his people discover us here."

"I'm sorry, I can't go. Not yet." I begged him with my eyes to understand. "I have to say goodbye to him. Don't leave without me."

Before he could say another word or attempt to stop me, I darted off across the plains as fast as my feet could carry me. I knew I risked much. Jekop was no doubt already furious. Saying goodbye would inspire many questions and probably cause an even greater rift between us. Speed was imperative to Slane. Lives were depending on his return. But I couldn't just leave. Not this way.

Though Jekop's tribe was of the plains, they were actually quite a distance from Stonehenge, although closer than they'd been when at the caves. The sacred area, as he called it, required a certain degree of deference, considering it was a meeting place of the gods. And since the gods didn't appreciate mere mortals meddling in their affairs, they wouldn't take kindly to an entire tribe crowding them. According to Jekop, Slane and his people had no regard for the gods' wishes. At least with Slane leaving, Jekop should be appeased. A peaceful resolution had been reached after all.

There was a patch of trees I had to cut through in order to reach Jekop's campground. Clouds were thick overhead, and when I reached the cover of the trees, the night became even blacker. I had to tread carefully now. Becoming tripped up would cost me more time. Slane had already expressed his impatience. I knew he wouldn't wait long. Just as I was about to break free onto the plains again, a large looming shape suddenly stepped out from behind a tree and blocked my path.

"Stop!" demanded a voice I recognized at once.

"Jekop? Oh, thank God!" I leaped into his arms, and he held me for a long moment before setting me back down. "I'm so sorry I left you at the caves. It was an emergency, though. Slane had to return."

"I thought he might have forced you to go with him. I went to his camp and did not see you."

"We did go there, and then we left. Please, Jekop, I have to tell you. Slane, he's leaving. And so am I."

"Leaving?"

The pain I heard in his voice ripped at my heart. "I have to go home."

"Why must you return?"

What could I say? What possible reason could I give to explain why I had to go home to my shell of a life and leave him? "I just do."

"You belong here. With me."

Then, a thought occurred to me. It was true I did need to leave. I wanted to make sure Slane made it back to his world. Plus, I couldn't just disappear from my time without a trace. But Slane had told me on our way to the portal that he was coming back. He'd made his decision to start his life over again in this period. That way, he'd be here to meet others from the future when they arrived and to get them settled. So why couldn't I come back? There was nothing keeping me in my world. Nothing preventing my return.

"Jekop, I must leave, but only for a while." Hopefully, getting Slane home and wrapping things up in my world should only take a few months. "I will come back."

"You will?"

"Yes. Slane will, too. We can all be together again."

He reached out and held me tight. "Soon,

okay?"

"I promise." But now I had to go. I pulled away from Jekop and reached up to touch his handsome face. "I love you."

"I love you, too," he said.

And then, before I changed my mind, I turned and ran. Back toward Stonehenge and Slane. Before I even reached the portal, I could see it was deserted. Not able to run anymore, I slowed and ascended the incline to stand at the center of the posts. There was no sign of anyone or anything. It was as though Slane and his men had never been.

Perhaps something had happened? Maybe Slane thought I wasn't coming back and decided to turn the portal on and leave without me? If it hadn't worked, then he would have returned to his camp. If it had worked... I didn't even want to imagine him leaving me behind.

I left the circle. It took me a while to locate Slane's camp due to the darkness. I pushed open the door of his hut and called out to him. Nothing.

I went door to door, shouting for an answer. All was silent.

Upset and exhausted, I returned to Slane's hut and lay down on his bed. He'd gone, but I could follow him. If anything, I should be relieved that the dance had worked. At least, I hoped it had. I closed my eyes and decided to rest for a moment. I would return to Stonehenge and go after Slane. But for now, I was just so tired. Unintentionally, I drifted off to sleep.

I awoke to the press of lusty lips on mine. I bolted up on the bed, almost knocking my assailant over. My gaze focused a moment later, and I relaxed. "Slane!"

"Before you go off on me, listen to what I have to say." He wrapped his arms around me and held me tight as though he could shush my words this way.

"You left me." He wasn't about to get off easy.

"I did, and I'm sorry. You have to understand, after you left, I began to worry. We didn't even know if the dance would open the portal, but *if* it did, I didn't know what would be waiting for us on the other side. If it could bring us there, I could go and check things out and then come back again." He paused and took a breath. "As it turned out, all was clear on the other side."

"There was no one there?" I had to ask.

"Didn't see a soul. Although, when we

first came to this world, it was the same."

"Until Jekop and his tribe mistook you for ghosts."

"Yes." He squeezed me and planted a kiss on the top of my head. "Now that I know the caves are there, I got the men set up in them. They were empty and it turns out a perfect place to stay while we begin to put the blue stones in place."

I smiled at the thought of the caves. "I told Jekop we were leaving. I also said we'd return." I looked at his face to gauge his reaction.

"You—you'd come back?"

"My place is with you and Jekop. I love both of you. You're my world."

He smiled and kissed my lips. "Sorry, it took me a while to return. I had to do the dance the original way to get back. Learning it was much easier with you around." His expression became more serious. "It will take a while to get back you know."

"Yes, I know. And when we reach my world I have to wrap some stuff up. You can pick me up there when you're ready, and then we can both return to Jekop."

"There's nothing I'd like more."

The depth of love for me I saw shining in

his eyes moved me. Slane had always seemed so cool and detached. I guess the fate of his world had plagued him. Now that he knew he could make it home, he let his guard down.

"Are you ready to leave with me?" he asked.

"Yes." The sooner we left, the sooner we would return. Over the next few months I could comfort myself with my memories and the knowledge that one day soon we'd all be together again. This time, forever.

* * * *

As I pen these last words, I also keep a close eye on the now deserted area around Stonehenge. The crowds began thinning as the sun set, and finally, I am alone, just as on that one fateful day when I'd waited for everyone to leave so I could fulfill my dream of dancing at the stones. I now await to fulfill another dream.

What remains of my life in this time now rests in a large sack at my side. This journal of mine is one of the few possessions I'll bring back with me. At any moment, I expect my love's return.

Setting the stones in place turned into quite an affair involving the help of many more people than we had with us. Thank goodness others were willing to help. Now that I had a hand in the creation of Stonehenge, its presence holds far more meaning. To me it will always represent the bringing of Jekop and Slane and I together. For that, I will be eternally grateful.

Though I hold the key to one of the greatest mysteries on Earth, its secrets will be safe with me. For who am I but one small speck in the history of time? If anyone questions my sudden disappearance, may I become just another of the world's mysteries.

There's a brief flash of light. From behind one of the stones, a man emerges.

My love has returned.

I close my eyes tight and silently say a heartfelt goodbye to this place, this time. Though not my first farewell, this will be my last one. Slane, Jekop, and I have another destiny to fulfill.

For me, my journey is just beginning.

THE TULPA
KNIGHT

PROLOGUE
THE TULPA KNIGHT

Kallie Evander's thoughts have made Jamie de Brock — the medieval villain from her romance novel — come to life. As unbelievable as it seems, she cannot fathom another possible explanation for the giant, handsome rogue she suddenly finds in her bedroom. Nor can she mistake the extreme attraction they have for one another. While their passion overtakes them, Kallie is not only consumed by lust but also with guilt. Jamie is a tulpa, a thought form that has been made real by her intense concentration. She fears he will eventually turn on her. So, while she lies in his arms and fights her growing love for him, she must also devise a way to destroy him…before it is too late.

CHAPTER 1

THE TULPA KNIGHT

"I have to go, Ash. Nick is gonna be here in under two hours, and I still have a lot to do."

Kallie bounced on one foot across the hardwood floor of her tiny, neat-as-a-pin apartment, trying desperately to shake off the dryer sheet that was sticking to her sock. Under her arm, she balanced the laundry basket precariously on her hip. In the other hand, she held the cordless phone. She'd heard the ringing as she struggled to unlock the door and rushed inside to make a mad grab. How disappointing it'd only been her best friend, Ashley. Then again, it was probably a good thing it *had* been her. It might have been Nick. And if it was, and he was calling this close to the 'final hour,' he could have been calling to back out. And there was no way she was gonna let that happen.

Too much hard work and high hopes had been invested in this night. She'd been cooking all day. All of Nick's favorites. The table had been set. The romantic retro CDs had been placed by the old-fashioned player. The candles rested in their candelabras, awaiting the perfect moment to be lit. And best of all was the sexy little backless dress she'd bought downtown. She'd prayed the entire time that no one she knew would walk into the store and ask what prim and proper Kallie Evander was doing buying something so scandalous.

"It's not too late to cancel, you know. You can still scrape some self-respect off the floor and tell that bum to F-off," Ash said over the phone.

Why couldn't she understand how important this was to Kallie? "Not all of us can be lucky enough to have a great guy like you've got, Ash."

"But you know what an ass Nick is. He cheated on you and broke your heart. Now you're willing to allow him to weasel his way back into your life?"

"That was two months ago. He's changed. I'm sure this time he's changed. I don't want to be alone anymore. Besides, you know all I've gone through to make this work out."

"Yes, and why is it, do you think, it has to be *you* who's making all the effort? You don't need him. You're a best-selling romance author! You know guys aren't supposed to behave like that."

"I can't talk about this anymore. I have to go. I'll call you tomorrow."

Before Ash could argue further, Kallie hung up the phone. She couldn't stand to hear any more negativity about this evening. She had enough doubts running around in her head as it was.

She tossed the phone down on the couch on her way to the bedroom then dumped the laundry basket out on her bed and placed it on the floor. It'd been so embarrassing doing her laundry downstairs. She was positive that old Mrs. Hanson had been staring at her g-string panties as she'd fished them out of the dryer. Those were something else she'd bought downtown when she'd picked up her dress. The salesgirl insisted she shouldn't ruin the effect with nasty old panty lines.

Kallie had tried them on for the briefest of seconds before peeling them off and adding them to the wash pile. She hated the way they felt between her butt cheeks, like a perma-wedgie. It was definitely going to be a long evening wearing those. But it would all be worth it in the end. When she and Nick finally retired to her bedroom to rekindle their romance.

She could almost imagine the shock and delight on his face when he saw her in those panties. All thoughts he'd had of her being the same old, boring Kallie would fly right out the window.

Feeling a little daring, Kallie began taking off her clothes. She still had some time before Nick came over, and she wanted to practice her sexy poses in the mirror some more. This time, she could try them while wearing the panties and see if she looked any better.

Once she'd stripped down to her bra, she searched through the clothes on the bed until she found a pair of the panties. She slipped them on and hiked up the waistband on her hips. She'd bought two pairs of black, figuring they'd probably go with just about anything. She turned around before the mirror and checked out her rear end. She was already feeling uncomfortable with that skinny strip of material between her legs and had to resist the urge to tug at it.

Don't think about it. Just ignore it.

The salesgirl had sworn they'd be easy to get used to, and after a couple of wears, she'd wonder how she ever got along without them.

But right now, it's all I can think of.

Maybe if I walk around a little, she thought, sauntering back and forth across the room. She again stepped before the full-length mirror and had to admit she did indeed look pretty sexy. Now, she just needed to work on her walk. She swung her hips from side to side as she sashayed around in what she was certain was a sexy jaunt. Then she tried a few poses before the mirror and even tried bending over to see how she looked. She noticed her nipples were hard and poking against the lace of her bra.

Either I'm turning myself on or it's colder in here than I thought.

Kallie walked out of her room and went to the thermostat in the hallway. She turned it up another five degrees, figuring if Nick got overly warm, it'd just be easier to get him out of his clothes. And getting him out of them was exactly what she had planned. If she could get him into her bed, she was certain she could revive their relationship.

How desperate are you?

"Oh, be quiet," she snapped at herself. "Once we're back together, things will be great again."

Yes, Nick will be his usual controlling self, telling me I shouldn't have a life while he goes out partying every night and cheats.

"No! This time will be different."

Sure it will. Yeah. Right.

Kallie stomped into the kitchen and checked on the dishes she had warming in the oven. Everything looked fine and would be perfect when Nick arrived. A little dry, perhaps, but at least she wouldn't be fumbling around in the kitchen, leaving him to fend for himself on the couch, getting bored while she cooked. That wouldn't do at all.

She practiced her walk on the way back to the bedroom. "There, you see? The panties are hardly bothering me at all now."

Before the mirror, she again practiced her poses and bending. She didn't want to get into her dress yet. With her luck, she'd spill something on it and would have to find a different outfit to wear. But she didn't want to don her sweats either, not when she was suddenly feeling so sexy.

She eyed the pile of clean clothes getting wrinkled on her bed and decided she'd better get that chore over with. Although, it might be kind of fun leaving them there so when Nick carried her into the bedroom, he could hold onto her with one muscular arm and use the other to sweep her clothes to the floor. Then, after they made mad, passionate love on the bed, they'd do it again on the nest of clothing on the floor.

Nah. Then I'll have to wash them all over again. She shrugged and began to fold.

After everything was tucked away in drawers and in the closet, Kallie dimmed the lights and again sexy-walked to the kitchen to make sure the two bottles of white wine she had in the fridge were sufficiently chilling. She went into the living room and dimmed the lights in there, too. Mood lighting. Then she started back to her bedroom, figuring she'd throw on a robe.

Suddenly, she stopped dead in her tracks. Rustling sounds were coming from her bedroom.

It couldn't possibly be an intruder. She was on the sixth floor, and her door was securely locked. At least, she was pretty sure she'd locked it. The phone had been ringing, and she'd been holding onto that laundry basket, so she couldn't be certain.

Kallie backed up and peered across the living room toward the door of her apartment.

It was shut. But that didn't mean anything. The intruder could have closed it. And even though she could see the lock was turned, he could have done that, too.

She crept silently up the hallway toward her bedroom, straining her ears for more sounds, but she didn't hear anything. Perhaps it'd been her imagination? After all, she was on edge. Plus, it was a crowded building. Maybe one of her neighbors was moving furniture around? Besides, she couldn't very well run out and yell for help. Not dressed the way she was. Or…undressed.

Taking no chances, she slipped into the kitchen and pulled out a long, sharp knife from the drawer, and then crept back down the hallway. Nothing seemed amiss in her room when she peered around the doorway. She suddenly felt very foolish, standing in her bra and panties, brandishing a butcher knife.

But what if she wasn't mistaken? What if someone was in her room? Or some*thing*? What if there was a mouse in there? Just last week she'd overheard a conversation on the elevator between Mrs. Alvas and her thirty-something-ish daughter talking about a mouse.

Well, if there was a mouse in there, she'd

give it a good scare. She took a flying leap into the middle of her bedroom floor, knife swinging menacingly, and let loose a loud, "Hi-yah!"

Before she knew what hit her, Kallie was disarmed of her weapon, and her feet swept out from beneath her. Then, she was lying flat on her back with a large sword aimed at her throat.

"What the hell!" she snarled, too angry to be scared. That was until she got a look at her assailant. When her eyes focused on the giant, bare-chested, medieval-looking warrior standing over her, she fainted dead away.

When Kallie awoke, she found herself in her bed with the covers tucked up under her chin. She relaxed and nestled securely into the down-filled pillow beneath her head and sighed. She'd been dreaming.

Yeah, that's it.

After folding her clothes and checking on the wine, she'd crawled into bed and had a little nap. That way, she'd be nice and rested for an exhausting, love-filled night with Nick.

Nick! She sat up in a hurry and stared at her alarm clock. He was due to arrive in less than forty minutes.

She flung back the covers and was about to leap from her bed when she heard a sound,

like someone clearing their throat, coming from
the corner of her room. *No!* She'd been napping.
She knew she had. That whole episode with a
giant, half-naked, sword-toting warrior had
been a dream. Hadn't it?

"My lady…"

Kallie's head snapped in the direction of
the voice. "Gaaa…"

"Nay, my lady. My name is Jamie."

"Wha…wha…what?"

"Are you ill?" He came over slowly to
the side of the bed and knelt down on the floor.
"I am sorry if I hurt you. You startled me."

She startled *him*?

Kallie leaped up and dashed to the other
side of the room, her gaze darting around
frantically for the knife she'd been holding.
When she failed to find it, she put her back
against the wall and held up her little fists.
"Don't come near me if you know what's good
for you!"

He raised an eyebrow at her. "What is
good for me?"

Was that a touch of sarcasm she noted in
his tone? "I'll have you know I'm a black belt."
She wasn't, but he didn't have to know that.

"Aye, I can see that you have a black

belt."

He was staring at her g-string panties. Kallie felt a mortified blush heat up her cheeks. She vaguely remembered hearing somewhere that if you find yourself about to be attacked, you should talk to your assailant. Make him see you as a person and not just the object of his vile intentions. "Your name is Jamie?"

He stood up and went to the end of the bed, taking a seat on the flung about covers. "Aye."

"Well, Jamie, my name is Kallie, and this is my apartment you're in. I'm sure it must be a mistake, and I'll be happy to show you the exit." Did that sound a little too forceful? She didn't want to make him angry, but she did want him to leave.

"Apart ment?"

"Yes, my apartment. You're in my apartment."

Was he simple? Or maybe he was drunk? And what was with the get-up he had on? If she didn't know better, she'd think he was there to audition for the cover of her new book.

Jamie rose to his feet and began to walk around the room, examining things. He touched everything he saw, lifting objects to peer at them closely, even putting them to his nose to sniff.

Kallie kept a watchful eye on him and waited for a chance to make a break for the doorway. Every time she inched closer to it, he repositioned himself as though aware of her intent. Suddenly, Jamie came to stand before her, holding an old trophy in his hands that she'd bought at a garage sale. He was eyeing her critically as though he knew she hadn't won first place in a soccer tournament. She'd been really close to winning one in high school. At least, she would have been if evil Beatrice hadn't tripped her up and made her look like an idiot during tryouts. If it hadn't been for Beatrice, she would have made the team, and when the Flying Falcons had taken first place, she would have been there to get a trophy of her own. Oh, how she hated Beatrice! That's why she'd given her name to the spoiled, nasty wife-to-be of one of the knights in her newest book. You know what they say about payback. And when you're a novelist, it can definitely be a bitch.

"This is from a tournament?" Jamie waved the trophy in front of her face.

"Yes, for soccer. See the little man kicking the ball?" She tried not to sound condescending, but what was with him?

"Sock her?"

Yep, he was drunk. "No. *Soccer.* There's no *her*. It's one word."

She didn't have time for this. Nick was going to be there soon, and if she had any chance of reconciling with him, she had to get this goon out of here. Although, she had to admit, now that she gazed at Jamie more closely, he was a handsome goon. He was huge and muscular but didn't seem quite so intimidating anymore. Not when he was looking at her with that little lost boy look on his face. He was actually kind of cute. She was almost five and a half feet tall, and he towered over her, so she guessed him to be about six-foot three or four. His hair brushed his shoulders in soft, dark waves, and she had to resist the urge to run her fingers through it. His eyes were so dark brown that they appeared almost black. A girl could get lost in those eyes, and that was no cliché.

What's the matter with me?

His scent was enticingly masculine, rugged, and natural, as if he'd just stepped out of a summer breeze that'd been blowing gently through the forest. Though he was a stranger, he also seemed so darned familiar.

"Have we met?" It seemed a strange

question, even to her ears. How could they have possibly met? Surely she would have remembered a rogue such as he?

"Nay," he said, although he appeared to ponder the possibility. "This place." He gestured around the room. "'Tis strange." He turned and walked back across the floor, taking a seat on her bed again.

She could have darted from the room while his guard was down, but something made her hesitate. "Why do you talk like that?"

"You speak strangely," he said at the same time.

Kallie smiled at him, and although his face was still grim, he gave her a tight smile in return.

"Jamie, do you know where you live?" Perhaps he'd hit his head or something?

"Aye. I hail from Tenebrous Castle."

Now she understood. Someone was playing a trick on her.

Ashley!

"All right." Kallie, angry now, stomped over to stand before him. "Enough of the acting, buddy. You can toddle back to Ash and tell her it's not going to work. I'm going through with this date with Nick, and no one is gonna stop me. You got that?"

He looked at her like she was speaking a different language. "Acting? Toddle through ash? Nick?"

"Yes! All those things. Now go. He'll be here soon."

"Who will be here?"

"Nick will be here." Why was he deliberately being obtuse? He knew the jig was up. "Just leave."

She grabbed onto one huge bicep and tried to pull him off the bed. He easily grabbed both of her hands, but she continued to shove at him with her body. As he tried to stop her futile attempts to move him, she was knocked off balance and wound up falling onto his lap. He immediately put his arms around her in a gallant attempt to stop her from sliding to the floor.

Kallie was again mortified. Sitting there on his lap in her lacy bra and panties. In *g-string* panties that allowed her bottom to uninhibitedly feel the muscles of his thighs through his tight pants.

Mercy!

Kallie honestly didn't know how or why, but she suddenly found herself leaning toward him. He leaned toward her, and their lips met in the most amazing, sizzling kiss she'd ever had from anyone in her entire life. Even Nick.

His lips were like fire against hers, and she felt herself falling and being devoured by flames all at the same time. It went on for ages, and every line from every book she'd ever read or written came to mind about passion-filled kisses that she thought only belonged in fiction. But there she was, living and breathing one. Her only coherent thought was *Wow*.

The next thing she knew, they were lying back on the bed, and her breasts sprang free of their lacy confines, and his hands were all over her at once. His pants magically fell away from his beautiful body. Though Kallie suspected her tugging hands had something to do with it. She felt the string between her butt cheeks being wrenched away effortlessly and caught a glimpse of black panties flying through the air. Then he was nestled between her open thighs and entering her. All she could do was groan in delight and satisfaction, despite the fact that the man on top of her was not her ex-boyfriend Nick, as she'd planned, but some medieval actor her best friend must have surely hired.

Kallie briefly entertained the thought

that he might be a gigolo because he certainly seemed to be a pro. He thrust in and out of her for long, agonizing minutes, watching her face the entire time, getting her into an absolute frenzy of mindless wanting. His hands squeezed her breasts, and his hot mouth latched onto her nipple, his teeth tugging and teasing the hard pebble. And when she felt her world explode, he waited until her pleasure was complete before he spilled his seed on her belly.

"Ah, it's nice to meet you, Jamie," was all she could think to say in the aftermath of their lovemaking.

"The pleasure is mine," he said, cuddling her closely against his chest.

"Not completely."

And when their lips met in another fiery kiss, and she felt him stir to life against her thigh, she heard the words she'd never forget as long as she lived.

"I'm not usually into threesomes, but if you're up for it, I'll give it a go," said Nick, who had chosen that moment to use his key to let himself into Kallie's apartment and find Jamie and her in this compromising situation.

It wasn't exactly the reunion she'd had in mind.

CHAPTER 2

THE TULPA KNIGHT

Kallie slammed the door so hard she thought it would shatter, but in that moment, she didn't care. It's not like she needed a heavy, wooden door anyhow, considering she now had a giant to protect her.

After Nick had surprised them and winked at her as though he didn't care a whit about what she was doing, Jamie had sprung out of bed in all his naked glory and physically removed him from the room. Before Nick could come to any great harm, she was able to run down the hall after the struggling pair while pulling on her hastily snatched robe. She finally hollered loud enough to get Jamie to release Nick's neck. Nick had glared at the both of them as he stumbled toward the front door, hissing out such scathing words she was surprised she was able to stop Jamie from finishing him off.

Kallie spun around and glared daggers at the man in her living room. "What the hell was that?"

Jamie recoiled as though she'd struck him. "He insulted you—us—with his vile suggestion!"

His remarkable chest was heaving, and a layer of sweat glistened all over his body. His manhood lay limp against his thigh, but as he caught her staring, it began to stir to life again. And as he became fully erect, she marveled over the fact that she'd actually fit that huge thing inside her body.

She had to get control of herself. All she could suddenly picture in her mind was laying down right where she stood and having him jump on top of her. When had she become so uninhibited when it came to sex? She'd never been like this before, not with anyone. Although, there was something different about Jamie. It was as if he wasn't real and was just some perverted figment of her imagination.

But it had taken more than a mere illusion to toss someone as big as Nick from her apartment. Now that she thought about it, she kind of liked the way Jamie had done that for her. No one had ever rushed to defend her honor like that before.

It reminded her of her newest romance

novel. The way her hero Merick had rushed to her heroine Melanie's defense against those alehouse scoundrels. And although poor, weak Merick had been soundly thrashed for his noble deed, he had at least attempted to be Melanie's champion. Kallie decided that's what turned her on so much about Jamie in that moment — the fact that he'd been her champion.

But as he walked toward her with his massive prick swinging to and fro and a heated look in his eye, she recalled the fact that he was in on this little sham with Ashley to divest her of any hopes of reconciliation with Nick. Which he had succeeded in doing.

Kallie's hands came up to brace against Jamie's chest as he moved before her. "Are you happy? Now you can run back to Ash and tell her the job is complete."

"What ash?" Jamie's eyes scanned the room as though looking for something. "This place is indeed strange, but I see no ash. There is not even a hearth."

He seemed to be battling with himself over the urge to nose about the room, as he'd done in her bedroom, or to giving his attention to his baser needs. His hardened rod lowered and pushed against the apex of her thighs like a heat-seeking missile. Kallie took a step back, wrapped her robe tightly around her, and tied the belt. It was hard for her to concentrate with his prick so close to its destination. Her body was becoming covered with a sheen of its own, and she had to lick her suddenly dry lips.

"I don't know why you're continuing to play this game," she said. "You've won. You and Ashley have won. Nick is gone, and frankly, I don't care if he ever comes back." As she walked into the kitchen and turned off the oven, she heard his reply.

"Who is Frank? Is he kin to Nick?"

Kallie returned to the living room and shook her head. As much as she wanted to berate Jamie, she could tell by his expression that he was truly baffled. She took his hand and led him over to the couch. They sat down side by side, she still holding his hand in hers. She wasn't sure where Ash had found Jamie or how she convinced him to play this role, but they must have plotted this out together. There was only one other person in the world right now who knew about her knight, Jamie de Brock, and that he lived in Tenebrous Castle. And that was Ashley.

Kallie had told Ash bits and pieces about

the new book she was working on. Her working title was *Defying the Dragon*. And although the story was centered on the conflict between Merick and Melanie, her protagonists, Kallie had somehow become fixated on Jamie — the villain who was aptly named 'Dragon' in her story.

The thing that confused her, though, was if Ash was going to play this little trick, why hadn't she hired someone to play the part of Merick? Why had she chosen Jamie instead? Kallie hadn't revealed how she had unexpectedly become enamored with the villain in this story, so how had Ash figured it out? Perhaps she *was* predictable? Leave it to her to become infatuated with a jerk, though. She seemed to have a penchant for doing that.

It was strange. The way she could conjure up Jamie so vividly in her mind. The way he walked, talked, rode a horse, swung a sword. She would swear she even knew his scent. All this, and she was only on chapter six. Jamie had kidnapped Melanie and ridden off with her. He'd then secured her away in the east tower of his castle, leaving Merick to think the pair had run off together. Little did Merick realize his precious Melanie was an unwilling hostage of the misguided brute, Jamie. Kallie knew that if Merick were real, his heart would belong to Melanie. But Jamie was free to love. Maybe that was the reason she'd fallen for him.

It was hard to concentrate and figure things out with Jamie sitting so close to her. He was naked and aroused, and she could easily be divested of her robe. Too easily. Their earlier lovemaking had been wonderful, and she couldn't help but imagine how it would be again.

Kallie glanced at him with heat in her eyes. He looked so much like how she pictured her knight, Jamie. It was uncanny. "Jamie," she said softly.

He turned to her at once. "Aye?"

"Tell me about Tenebrous." This would slip him up. He wouldn't be prepared for this question. And after he stopped playing games with her, perhaps they could have a glass of wine, and he could tell her who he *really* was.

Instead of getting a panicked look on his face as she'd expected, Jamie became animated. He had a far-off look in his eyes, and his lips turned up into a charming smile. "Ahh, home." He sighed. "'Tis strange. One moment, I had kidnapped fair Melanie and brought her to my home to wed, and the next moment, I was here."

"Yes, but tell me what Tenebrous is like." Kallie ignored the tinge of jealousy she suddenly experienced, thinking about the *fair* Melanie nestled away in Tenebrous, awaiting Jamie's attention. She had a vivid image of the fictional castle in her mind, but she'd told no one about it.

"I had been over in France a year earlier with the young prince, and when I returned, 'twas gifted to me by his father, King Edward."

Of course, Kallie knew who had given him the castle, but she could have told Ash about that. Or perhaps he was a bit of a mind reader? He was good. She'd give him that. "Go on."

Jamie regarded her for a moment, then continued, "Well, 'tis square in shape and has five levels to it. There are four towers, each with a fair-sized room at their peak. Perfect for *guests*. 'Tis where fair Melanie now awaits me. In the east tower, to be exact. It also sits upon a hill, which is strategic, but I am afraid it does live up to the name Tenebrous, for 'tis a dark and gloomy place."

"I see."

"Needs a woman's touch, I think. 'Tis

practically bare inside."

Kallie stood up and stomped her foot. "That's enough!"

Jamie shrugged his shoulders. "Whatever you wish. You did ask me."

Kallie began to pace back and forth across the room. This didn't make any sense to her. Jamie just described the castle that was in her mind *exactly*. She thought about what he'd said and rounded on him. "If *fair* Melanie awaits you to wed her, why did you and me just…"

He smiled like a rogue. "You are quite appealing, especially when you are angry."

What was she expecting? She had written him as a villain. "Wait a minute. Wait a minute." Was she actually beginning to believe that he was her Jamie? What was wrong with her?

Jamie rose to his feet and went to take her into his arms. "There now, are you jealous? Lady Melanie does not mean anything to me. 'Tis only her rich dowry that entices me."

"I had been thinking you were in need of money and looking to marry an heiress," Kallie conceded.

She rested her head on his chest and inhaled his masculine scent. He smelled so good and felt so right. So what if he was playing a part? Expertly. Or perhaps, she thought, tilting her head back and staring at him dreamily, maybe he was real?

"Are you real, Jamie de Brock? Did you jump out of the pages of my book and become true to life, flesh and blood?"

Jamie lowered his head to kiss her lips. "I know of no book," he murmured. "I do know that I desire you."

Kallie could feel the proof of his desire, boldly pressing up against her robe, trying to gain entrance. *Ah, why not?* Taking him into one hand, she parted her robe with the other and guided him toward his destination. Jamie lowered her to the floor and then spread her robe wide to gain access to her body. She could ponder the reason for Jamie's presence later. But now…now she wanted him to make love to her again.

Jamie's kisses began at her neck and then trailed down to her breasts, where he lingered for a while. Grasping handfuls of his soft, thick hair, Kallie contemplated the Jamie in her book. In the beginning, she'd thought to make him a self-serving, cruel man that her hero Merick had to rescue his beloved Melanie from, but something had changed. Somewhere along the line, as the chapters began unfolding on the pages, she had come to know and understand Jamie. He was a loner, almost an outcast. She could relate to that.

His kisses were now close to her belly, and Kallie wondered if he'd stop there. Nick had never gone down *there* during their lovemaking, always selfishly seeking his fulfillment in a hurry. He had seemed to enjoy her ministrations on him, but he also had a way of making her feel inadequate. She remembered he wasn't quite as endowed as Jamie was. Just thinking about Jamie inside of her...how large and overwhelming he'd been...

Suddenly, her hips lifted off the floor as she felt his tongue upon her moist center. Hearing a soft chuckle from the giant between her legs, Kallie laid back and tried to relax. She didn't want him to realize how inexperienced she was. But then she felt one large finger slip inside her.

"Ohhh." The word slipped past her lips before she could stop it.

"Aye, sweetheart," Jamie encouraged before lowering his lips to her again.

Kallie's head began to thrash from side to side. She couldn't control it. She was too busy keeping control over the gasps and moans trying to escape her mouth. But when she felt another of his fingers slip within her, she came undone.

"Oh gawd! Yes, yes, yes."

With his mouth still on her, Jamie's other hand reached beneath her to cup her bottom and give it a squeeze. He held her steady so she could not unintentionally wriggle away from him as she thrashed about. Just as she was about to burst, he suddenly stopped.

"No! Don't stop now."

Jamie moved his body up over her, keeping himself between her thighs. He reached down and tossed one of her legs over his hip and did the same with the other one. Then he entered her with agonizing slowness.

Kallie tried to rise up to him, but Jamie would have none of that. He stilled her motions by lifting his hips and withdrawing from her until she ceased her actions. When she cried out in frustration, he silenced her with a kiss. His tongue entered her mouth and danced within while his lower region crept slowly forward.

Kallie suckled on his tongue desperately and dug her heels into his back. She'd never known such torment. It seemed to take forever for him to finally reach his destination, and when he did, he remained still. Just when Kallie feared she would beg, he began to move. Sliding almost right back out, he again pushed forward. This continued, while each time, his thrusts became faster and faster. Kallie moved her hips up to meet him, her breath coming out in gasps. She'd never known such intensity before, never surrendered herself so completely. Finally, they met their peak together, each crying out their pleasure.

Afterward, Jamie carried her off to the bedroom, and Kallie fell asleep, nestled in the safety of his arms.

* * * *

The bright sunshine beating down on her face through the window urged Kallie to awaken. She stretched slowly, sensually, feeling more content than she'd felt in a very long while. When her hand came in contact with hard muscles, she paused for a moment and then smiled. She turned on her side and looked longingly at the rugged man beside her.

"Good morn to you," Jamie said, a lazy smile on his face.

"And to you." Over his broad shoulder, Kallie could see the long, heavy broadsword leaning against the bedroom wall. She puzzled at it for a moment.

Seeing the direction of her gaze, Jamie turned to look at what had her so intrigued. "Does the lady wish to handle my sword?" His eyebrows wiggled at her suggestively.

"Very funny." Kallie climbed over him and went to kneel down before the weapon.

When she reached out to carefully touch it, she heard Jamie say, "I meant—"

"I know what you meant!" Kallie interrupted. "Wow, I can't believe the craftsmanship of this. It really looks like it's from the fourteenth century."

"'Tis from the year of our Lord 1345, to be exact. I had it crafted two years ago."

Kallie's head snapped back to the bed. "What did you say?"

"I said I had it crafted two years—"

She got to her feet. "My novel takes place in 1347. I didn't tell Ash that. How did you know?"

"Ash again."

"Yes! Ash again. My friend, Ashley. Remember her? The one you concocted this little ruse with."

Kallie moved closer and regarded him

carefully. Now, in the light of day, she gave his body her full scrutiny. Last night, she'd been so overcome with emotions. First being shock, then lust, then mortification, then anger, confusion, surprise, and then anger again. Then lust. And more lust. She'd failed to really notice the scars that marred Jamie's beautiful body. It was quite surprising, she realized, considering the amount he had. She traced her finger down a long, jagged scar that stretched from his shoulder to his elbow.

"Crécy," Jamie said.

"Pardon?"

"In France. The battle of Crécy. 'Twas a long sword." Jamie turned and showed her a wound about the size of a silver dollar on the back of his shoulder. He then pointed to a larger, healed-over gash on the front side. "Arrow. Went right through, after a bit of yanking by my second." He turned to show her the back of his leg. "Morning Star. That unlucky fellow did not survive the blow I gave him in retaliation."

Kallie had to work to keep her mouth from dropping open during Jamie's inventory of battle wounds. She was well versed in the machinations of medieval weaponry, but not too often did she meet another who was. "Your second?"

"Aye, Tristan. I wonder where he is now."

Involuntarily, Kallie took a step back. "*No one* knows that!"

"Aye, I suppose not. I do not even know where *I* am."

"No! I mean, no one knows your second's name is Tristan! I haven't even written it down yet. It's only been in my mind."

Jamie looked at her with concern. "Are you all right, Kallie?"

It was the first time he'd said her name, and it sounded strange. "It's Kallasandra, actually." She didn't know why it mattered whether he knew her name or not.

"Kallasandra." He smiled after he said it as though giving his approval.

When he patted the spot beside him on the bed, Kallie sat down. She suddenly felt drained as the realization hit her. Jamie was real!

Her Jamie. Jamie de Brock, the villain from her novel, was real. Somehow, someway, defying all reason, he was here. She dropped her head into her hands. "I feel dizzy."

Taking her into his arms, Jamie comforted

her. "We will figure this out."

Kallie basked in his strength for a moment, then reluctantly rose to her feet. "I'm gonna take a shower. When I'm done you can have one, then we'll sit and have a big pot of coffee and talk."

She didn't wait for him to reply. Standing in the shower moments later, as the hot water ran over her, she scrubbed at her face and wondered if she should laugh or cry. She'd either lost her mind, or the unimaginable had happened to her.

CHAPTER 3

THE TULPA KNIGHT

A tulpa! That's what Jamie is, a tulpa.

Kallie sat at the tiny kitchen table with a large cup of coffee before her. After showing Jamie how to use the bathroom facilities, she'd put on a pot of coffee to brew and grabbed her laptop.

She spent a while searching the internet before stumbling upon this strange phenomenon.

Apparently, a woman had spent some time with Tibetan Monks and conjured up a little monk of her own just by the power of intense thought. There was even a book written about her experience. The frightening thing was she had lost control of the little fellow. Over time, her tulpa began to take on a form of its own. It no longer did her bidding and even became quite malevolent. It took her a long time and a lot more intense concentration to make the tulpa disappear.

When Jamie appeared in the kitchen wearing nothing but a towel, Kallie eyed him suspiciously. Would he, too, turn on her, just like the tulpa she'd read about? It seemed to be an occupational hazard as far as creating these creatures went. There'd been dozens of people online who stated they'd actually created tulpas of their own. Each time, the person reported the same thing—the tulpa became uncontrollable and had to be destroyed. Although it sounded like a bunch of malarkey, it was the only somewhat logical explanation of what she herself was experiencing.

Jamie took a seat at the table, and Kallie grabbed a mug. "Would you like cream and sugar? I usually just take mine black."

"I do not know how I like it." Jamie watched her pour the steaming black liquid into a mug. "You have such luxury here, in this place." He gestured around the kitchen.

Kallie placed the mug in front of him and sat down. Jamie placed his hands around the mug then bent down to sniff the contents.

"It has a strong aroma, but I find it strangely compelling." He lifted the mug to his lips and sipped. "'Tis good. It must be highly coveted?"

Kallie chuckled. "You've no idea. And that's just plain java without all the fancy frou-frou you can add to it."

"Frou-frou?"

They shared a laugh. It all seemed so normal. Sitting at the table, drinking coffee. Just as thousands of other people were spending their mornings. Kallie reminded herself that Jamie wasn't like other people. In fact, he really wasn't a person at all. Certainly, he looked and felt real enough, but that could change at any moment. Soon, he might grow fangs or claws and stalk out on his own to wreak havoc upon the town. She had to do something before she lost control of him.

She had to think him away.

The thought was very unpleasant. Jamie had been nothing but a complete gentleman since he'd been there, despite her creating him as a villain. He didn't act like a villain. And as he suddenly stood and nonchalantly stretched, and the towel that was balancing precariously on his hips fell to the floor, Kallie had to admit he was quite wonderful. She drank in the sight of his naked body. Scars and all, he was exquisite. And oh, so tempting.

He reached out his hand to her and she

felt herself floating into his embrace. Instead of carrying her off to the bedroom as she expected, she was surprised when he removed her laptop and the two mugs from the table and then lifted her up to place her bottom on the smooth, cool surface. Thank goodness it was a sturdy little square table with four strong legs.

He opened her robe and then spread her legs wide as he knelt before her. When he lowered his head to the heart of her sex, Kallie wasn't sure if she was to be the main course or dessert. She leaned back on her elbows and lifted her hips to him wantonly. Tomorrow be damned. She had plenty of time to think Jamie away before he became dangerous. Today, she would spend delighting in the arms of her creation.

"Yes!" The word escaped her lips before she could stop it. While she'd been deciding to put off her responsibilities, Jamie had slipped one of his fingers into her sheath.

After a few minutes of tormenting her with his mouth and fingers, he flipped her over on the table. Kallie held on as Jamie grasped her hips and lifted her bottom. In one swift plunge, he entered her. With fast, deep strokes, he took her to the brink of ecstasy, where she screamed her release. Jamie yelled out as pleasure claimed him as well.

* * * *

Hours later, Jamie held onto the dashboard of Kallie's car for dear life as she drove them out of town. She'd decided the best place to give her full attention to Jamie and his demise would be at the lake house she owned. It was only a two-hour drive to the cozy, isolated cabin, but with Jamie panicking every ten minutes or so and her having to slow the car to a crawl, it took over three hours to reach their destination.

After she parked the car, Kallie dropped her head onto the steering wheel. Jamie leaped out the door as fast as he could. So much for the fearless warrior she'd written him to be. She took a moment to calm herself before she got out and retrieved her bags from the trunk. As she struggled toward the door, Jamie finally came to his senses and helped her.

She unlocked the door and pushed it open, allowing him to go inside before her. He poked his head in cautiously before fully stepping in.

"'Tis safe." He moved aside and let her enter.

"I know it's safe," Kallie snapped. "It's

my cabin. No one's been here for over two years."

As he had in her apartment, Jamie walked around staring at things, full of curiosity. It didn't take him long to drop the bags he carried and start touching and sniffing everything. Kallie let him be and walked down to the larger of the two bedrooms and put her suitcase on the bed. She unpacked her clothes, putting them in the dresser, and laid her cosmetics and hairbrush on top of it. Then she unpacked the toiletries in the bathroom.

The cabin smelled stale after years of being neglected. She went around window to window, flinging them open. Finally, she was able to locate Jamie, who had found his way onto the deck and was staring out at the view of the lake. Kallie noticed the grass was in desperate need of cutting. The lake looked peaceful and quiet, and a feeling of calm contentment washed over her.

"Do you like it here?" she asked.

"Aye. Better than the busy town and all those vickles everywhere."

"Vehicles. Yes, I suppose you're right. Town can get hectic, but I get caught up with work and the convenience of being able to walk to the store."

"Do you harvest crops here, or is there a market nearby?"

Kallie smiled at him. "Yes, there's a market. A little village, actually. Remember we passed it about twenty miles away?"

"Nay, I believe I still had my eyes shut. It made traveling at such speed easier to bear."

His words sounded sarcastic, and Kallie had to remind herself to take it easy on him. She'd written him to be from the fourteenth century, where things weren't quite so modern. It must be terribly difficult for him to suddenly find himself in such an advanced society. Where he came from, things were handled by might. He was a powerful lord, a champion of King Edward's. Now, he was lost and probably frightened, which must be alien to him. It also didn't help that he had to rely on a female for his survival. Which reminded her, she held his very existence in her hands. Or rather, in her mind.

Kallie eyed him as he leaned on the rail of the deck and inhaled the scent of pine. According to everything she'd read online about tulpas, it could take anywhere from a couple of days to a couple of weeks for Jamie to begin to show signs of wickedness. So far, the only time he'd been a beast was when he was tormenting her during lovemaking.

The little rumble in Kallie's stomach reminded her that it was after noon and she hadn't eaten today. She'd packed supplies from home, knowing stopping to shop might prove difficult. If it took longer than a couple of days to vanquish Jamie, she would have to make a trip into town.

It was a good thing she could still go online, and her cellphone was receiving a signal. If she needed tips on increasing her concentration power she could find it via the internet. Or, if Jamie turned into a full-blown monster, she could call the sheriff. Concentrating him away was really her only option. She'd made this mess, and it was up to her to clean it up.

"Hungry?" she asked, getting Jamie's attention.

"Aye. You?" When Kallie nodded, he said, "I can hunt for something for us to eat."

"No. I, ah, brought stuff from the apartment. I'll make us something. How about some sandwiches?"

When Jamie winced, she elaborated. "Meat and cheese. On bread."

"All right."

She sighed as she went inside. This was going to be a long day.

* * * *

Two weeks of heavy concentration had gotten Kallie nowhere. After the second day at the cabin, she'd taken to spending a few hours a day working on her novel. She had a deadline for the end of August, and she needed to get busy. Unfortunately, the more she wrote about Jamie, the more she thought about him, which made her think she was unintentionally undoing any progress she'd made at getting rid of him.

Even if she did manage to get rid of him, what would stop him from reappearing as soon as she thought about him again? Ditching her book wasn't an option. After all, Merick and Melanie felt as real to her as Jamie despite them not appearing before her. And how could she possibly leave poor Melanie locked away in the east tower of Jamie's castle without any hope of rescue? Oh, the power she possessed in her hands. The responsibility.

It also didn't help matters any that Jamie, walking around all day in various stages of undress, was a huge distraction. Always wanting to make love to her. On the deck. On a raft in the water. In every room of the cabin. The possibilities were endless.

As she printed off her latest chapter on her handy-dandy portable printer, Jamie strolled into the smaller bedroom she'd set up as a makeshift office. "Is the noise freaking you out again?"

Jamie eyed the paper that hummed out of the machine magically covered with perfect little words and shrugged. "I am growing accustomed to it."

"Are the fish biting?" She'd shown him how to use her fishing rod, and once he'd gotten used to casting, he spent the majority of his time at the end of the dock stockpiling them with fish. In the evenings, he built up a fire in the pit and insisted on cooking the fish for dinner. She hadn't allowed him to hunt for any game, but fishing appeared to appease his manly desire to be the provider.

"I have three large bass for our dinner, my lady," he said, suddenly taking her into his arms.

"Oh no!" Kallie tried to catch the last paper that was streaming out before it fell to the floor. She struggled out of Jamie's embrace and made a mad grab for it then placed it on the neat pile she'd made on the spare bed.

"What is this book you care so much about?"

Although she'd talked to him about her novel when they'd been at the apartment, she didn't want to get into details about him being the villain in her story. She also didn't have the heart to tell him how he came to be in her world. He asked questions here and there, but she had neatly avoided them, telling him to just enjoy the time they had together. He hadn't pressed her for answers, which had been a relief. Mostly, he just seemed to care about living life, spending time doing what he loved to do—fishing and making endless love to her. And now, he had that heated look in his eye again.

"You're insatiable." Kallie laughed as Jamie began peeling off her clothing.

"And you, my lovely lady, are irresistible."

Ah, yes. She was definitely going to miss this rogue. Kallie allowed him to lower her to the thick carpet on the floor by the bed. She had piles of papers scattered about the room. She'd even made a pile on the dresser that contained similar cases to what she was experiencing, along with notes about how to increase her concentration so that she could be rid of her large problem.

As Jamie thrust inside her, Kallie's gaze traveled up to the notes she had handwritten and placed beside her printed stack of case papers. Since she'd wrapped up another chapter on her book, she felt that she could dedicate the rest of the week to concentrating on making Jamie vanish.

"Do you like that, Kallasandra?" he whispered seductively in her ear as he moved within her with slow, easy strokes.

"Yes." Being with him was wonderful and terrible at the same time. Every moment they spent together, she grew closer to him. She thought she knew everything there was to know about him, but as the days and nights went on, she found she was learning more and more. And she liked what she learned. He was kind and gentle, and noble. His presence was commanding and comforting at the same time. She loved the way he looked when he slept or ate or fished. She loved the easy way they could just be together.

She didn't love how much she was becoming attached to him. Too much so. She knew she had to end this as soon as possible.

* * * *

That night, Kallie lay wrapped in Jamie's arms in a nest of blankets on the deck, looking up at the starry night.

"Quick! Make a wish," she said, seeing a star shoot across the dark sky.

"I wish I could show you my home."

He sounded homesick, and Kallie was surprised. "Don't you like it here?"

He shifted to lean on his elbow and looked down at her. "Aye. I do. I like being with you. But I fear what is happening at Tenebrous in my absence. My men will be wondering where I am."

"Not to mention the lovely Melanie," Kallie said drolly.

Jamie laughed. "You are jealous."

"I am not." She tried to appear indignant but couldn't keep a stern face when Jamie suddenly bent down to nuzzle her neck.

"Little fool," he said gently. "Do you not know I have fallen in love with you? You have nothing to be jealous of. I will set Lady Melanie free as soon as I return home."

Kallie sat up with a start, her eyes bulging at Jamie. "You what?"

"I said I will set Lady Melanie free. 'Twas

wrong of me to take her."

"No! What else did you say to me?" Kallie stared into Jamie's beautiful eyes as they sat there wearing not a stitch of clothing. He'd just made love to her for hours after they'd eaten fish again for dinner. Between all the sweet berries she'd been finding and all the fish Jamie had caught, she didn't think she would ever have to make a trip into town.

Jamie took her face in both his hands and kissed her gently on the lips. "I said I love you, Kallasandra. Is that so hard to accept?"

"I..." She what? What could she say to that? *I'm beginning to love you, too, but at the same time, I'm also desperately trying to make you disappear forever before you turn into a monster?*

But he hadn't turned into a monster. In fact, the only changing he'd done had been for the better. He was not so arrogant anymore, and she'd even noticed how he respected her privacy if she was busy working. He was quick to learn about her world and accept and appreciate the modern conveniences. But was it enough? Could she leave things the way they were and just hope that he didn't change for the worse?

"Jamie, what if you could never go home? Would it be so terrible for you if you had to stay here in this world with me?"

He smiled at her and caressed her cheek. "Nay. I would miss my home, my world. But if I was to choose between returning there and losing you or staying here and having you, I would choose you."

Kallie felt a tear slip down her cheek. "I do love you, Jamie de Brock." She wrapped her arms around him, and their lips met as he lowered her to the blankets.

CHAPTER 4
THE TULPA KNIGHT

Kallie ran inside the cabin to grab a towel. After last night's revelations, she felt as though she had a whole new lease on life, and this morning, she was in the mood for a cool, refreshing swim.

"Jamie! Where are you? Do you want to jump in the lake with me? I stuck my foot in, and it's actually not so..." She stopped dead in her tracks outside the doorway of the spare bedroom. Jamie stood before the window, and in his hands, he held the printed pages of her manuscript. When he turned to regard her with an intense stare, she took a step back. "What are you doing?"

"Reading. I am quite capable of it, you know."

His voice was devoid of emotion, and Kallie felt as though she'd been submerged in ice water. "I know you can read. Let me explain."

Jamie held up a hand to halt her words. "Nay. I have seen everything."

He gestured to the handmade notes on the dresser, and Kallie cursed herself for not thinking to burn them. She hadn't imagined that Jamie would ever show an interest in what she wrote. But then again, why wouldn't he? He wasn't Nick.

"This explains my reason for being in this place." He rattled the chapters of her manuscript before him. "You made me up."

"No, Jamie, I…"

"And these." He dropped the papers he held and reached for her notes. "These talk about a tulpa. An imaginary being brought into existence by intense thought. You wrote about me. Created me as a character in your book, and I became real."

Kallie went to touch him, but he moved away from her. "Damn my book! Please, Jamie, it doesn't matter."

"I am not real." As the anguished words tore from him, Kallie could see his skin become translucent. She stepped closer but refrained from touching him, afraid her hand would slip through his if she tried to grasp it.

"Stop it! You're as real as I am. As real as anyone else."

He smiled ruefully. "I do not believe

anymore."

This time, she did snatch his hand, and although her grip was tenuous, she continued to hold him. "Don't you see, Jamie? All this time, I thought it was me who was keeping you here. *My* belief in you. But I was wrong. And *you* are wrong. It was never my belief. It was yours. You wanted to stay here with me."

"I am nothing more than a character in your book. A villain."

Kallie brushed away a cursed tear that stole down her cheek. "No. You are so much more than that. To me, you are everything. I brought you into being because I longed for you so much. I knew your name, I knew your voice, I knew how your skin felt against mine. Even before you appeared before me, I knew you, Jamie. Every part of you. I need you. Please don't leave me."

He pulled away easily. "You tried to get rid of me."

"At first! I admit I did. I was scared. From what I've read about similar circumstances things never turned out for the better. But then, as I got to know you, all that changed. I saw you evolve into a man whose strength and intelligence I admire. I saw you become a man

I could fall in love with. A man I *have* fallen in love with."

Jamie looked at her. "How can I change the fact that I am not a real man? I could never be what you want me to be. Not when I could just disappear at any moment."

Kallie saw him fade even more from her sight. "No!"

But it was too late. He was gone.

* * * *

It was the last week of August, and right on her deadline, Kallie wrote the final words of her novel. Since Jamie had disappeared, she had thrown herself into writing it, day and night, barely taking a break. And when she did sink into bed, in the wee hours of the morning, Jamie was on her mind. Try as she might, she could not make him reappear. She'd begun to think she imagined him. Imagined his touch, his kiss, his breath on her cheek, and her head on his chest as she slept. The pain was overwhelming. The loneliness was worse.

After printing off the last chapter of her manuscript, Kallie made the trip into town and mailed it off to her editor. She now had no reason to stay here. Her book was complete, and the summer was over. Most of the cottagers had already packed up and headed home, back to their lives, as should she. She'd done what she had intended to do — get rid of Jamie.

It was for the best, she told herself over and over. But at the end of each day, she would take a short break and sit on the dock to watch the sunset just as she and Jamie had done. "Come back to me," she'd whisper, the soft breeze taking her words and hopes along with it.

She knew she had to snap out of the funk she was in. She did not need a man to define who she was. She knew that now. She also knew that she would never settle for someone like Nick ever again. Jamie had taught her to respect herself. She didn't have to change for Jamie. He loved her the way she was. Quirks and all.

Now, as she sat once more at the end of the dock and waited for the sun to disappear, Kallie resolved to stand on her own. She got to her feet. Jamie wouldn't want her to sit around moping and feeling sorry for herself. He would want her to grab onto life with both hands and live like there was no tomorrow.

Kallie shook her fist in the air just like Scarlett O'Hara in *Gone With the Wind*, her favorite movie. Scarlett had loved Rhett, but when she lost him, she had carried on. She prevailed. *And so will I!*

The cabin was dark as she entered it, and Kallie had to stumble around and try to find the light. She would have sworn the lamp was only four steps from the door. She heard a noise.

She banged her toe on the edge of the end table just as she found the light. *Crash!*

"Great." The crash wasn't the only noise she heard. There'd been a slight rustling coming from down the hallway that sounded just like little mice when they thought no one was about. Kallie stumbled over to the light switch in the kitchen and flicked it on. She scooped up her shoe as she ventured down the hall. She had every intention of scaring the heck out of the little buggers.

As she stood outside her room waiting to leap within, she couldn't help but remember this was how she had first come to see Jamie. Her heart began to hammer in her chest. Maybe he had returned to her? Maybe it wasn't a mouse but it was Jamie making that rustling noise? Kallie dropped her shoe and leaped into the room.

"Jamie?" The hopeful cry tore from her lips.

One moment, she was standing in the middle of the room. The next, she was laying flat on her back. Kallie closed her eyes and took a deep, painful breath. Everything hurt. Though she had hit the floor hard, it felt as though she'd fallen farther than just a few feet.

She peeked open one eye and looked at the ceiling. But as her sight came into focus, the other eye opened, disbelieving in what she saw. Instead of the dusty ceiling fan she should be staring at, she saw what looked to be heavy wooden beams. As her eyes traveled down to the wall, she saw what suspiciously appeared to be a tapestry.

"Are you going to lie there all day, Kallasandra?" came a deep voice from behind her head.

Kallie sat up and quickly spun around, ignoring the pain in her head. "Jamie?"

Standing there, dressed from head to toe in medieval garb, was the man of her dreams. In his hand, he held a parchment, still wet with ink. Letting the papers fall to the floor, Jamie knelt down to take her into his arms. He kissed her lips and then lifted her with ease, carrying her over to the huge bed that sat high upon a platform and had heavy curtains that could be closed to conceal its occupants.

"Your head will take only a moment or two to clear if I remember correctly." Jamie placed her gently on the soft quilt and sat down beside her on the edge of the bed.

"Jamie, I don't understand. How did I get here? *Where* is here?"

He gestured to the parchment that lay on the wooden floor. "I wrote about you. Everything I could think of. I thought about you very hard every day. And now, you are here."

"*You* brought me to you?"

"Aye." He kissed her lips once more.

"But this isn't real! This is my story. Are you telling me we're in a *book*?"

"Who is to say what is real and what is not? And who is real and who is not? Can we not just be together, be it here or in your world?"

"But what if I vanish just as you did?" she said, grasping onto Jamie's shirt lest she suddenly slip away.

"You must believe. Believe in me, believe in *us*."

Kallie wrapped her arms around him and held him tight. "I love you, Jamie, with all my heart. This is what I know to be real. I believe in our love and that it will always bring us together, no matter where we are."

Jamie bent down his head and kissed her gently. "And I love you, my Kallasandra. We will always be one," he vowed before lowering her to the bed and making sweet love to her all night long.

Juliet is an award-winning author of several best-selling novels and short stories. She lives in Ontario with her husband, cat and dog. You can check out Juliet's website to see what she's been up to.
http://JulietCardinWebsite.Yolasite.com